A
BRUSH
with
DEATH

A SMALL TOWN COZY MYSTERY

Violet Brooks

About the Author

Violet Brooks is an author of cozy mysteries and sweet romances that transport readers to charming worlds brimming with warmth, intrigue, and heart. A resident of South Florida, Violet enjoys weaving tales of love and mystery that offer a perfect escape from the everyday.

When she's not writing, Violet spends her time reading and painting, two passions that inspire her creativity. She shares her home with two affectionate cats who keep her company during her writing sessions and provide endless entertainment.

Whether it's solving a curious whodunit or discovering the spark of new love, Violet's stories invite readers to slow down, savor the moment, and lose themselves in captivating, feel-good adventures.

Chapter 1

Lila's brow creased in concentration as she added the final brushstrokes to her painting, her blue eyes locked on the canvas. Swirls of color appeared beneath her brush.

The door to her studio creaked open. Lila glanced up to see Samantha's chestnut hair poke through the door. The rest of her entered, balancing a tray with two steaming cups of coffee and pastries from the local coffee shop. The rich aroma filled the air, bringing a smile to Lila's lips.

"You're a lifesaver, Sam," Lila said, setting down her brush and palette. She stretched, rolling her stiff shoulders and brushing back her blond hair. "I've been at this for hours. I need to stop before I ruin it."

"I figured you could use a pick me up." Samantha handed her a mug, the warmth seeping into Lila's paint-flecked hands. "This new work is absolutely stunning, Lila. The attention to detail is mind-blowing."

Lila took a sip, savoring the bold flavor. As her blue eyes traced the intricate details of the painting, she couldn't help but feel as though the colors and shapes were constantly shifting and morphing before her. It was her most ambitious work yet, one she hoped would be the centerpiece of her upcoming show at Evelyn's gallery.

But a flicker of nervousness passed through her at the thought of Evelyn. Lila's stomach fluttered with a mix of excitement and nerves. Evelyn's faith in her friend's work had always been a driving force, pushing her to explore new depths in her art. But lately, the pressure to live up to those expectations had begun to weigh on her. She pushed the thought aside, not wanting to dwell on her insecurities.

"I just hope it measures up to Evelyn's expectations," Lila said, voicing the doubt. "This show means everything."

"Are you kidding? Evelyn's going to love it. She adores your work, Lila. We all do."

Lila managed a smile, bolstered by her friend's unwavering faith in her. She knew she was lucky to have

Samantha in her corner, especially after the turmoil of her recent divorce had left her feeling mistrustful.

Lila turned to face her friend, a smile playing at the corners of her lips. "You really think so?"

"Without a doubt. Your talent never ceases to amaze me." Samantha reached out and gave Lila's paint-covered hand a gentle squeeze. "Evelyn is going to be thrilled to showcase this at the gallery. It's going to be the talk of the show."

A flicker of uncertainty crossed Lila's face. She glanced back at the painting, scrutinizing every detail. "I hope you're right," Lila said, her voice tinged with a mix of hope and apprehension. She took another sip of coffee, letting the warmth spread through her.

As if sensing her doubts, Samantha's voice softened. "Hey, don't go second-guessing yourself now. This piece is brilliant, Lila. Trust me."

Lila met Samantha's brown gaze, finding reassurance in her friend's soft features and unwavering support. "I don't know what I'd do without you, Sam. You've been my rock through everything—especially with the divorce and all. I don't think I could have made it through without you."

"That's what best friends are for." Samantha's smile was warm and genuine. "I'll always be here to cheer you on and bring you copious amounts of caffeine."

Laughter bubbled up in Lila's chest, the tension in her shoulders easing. "Speaking of which, this coffee is divine. You're an absolute lifesaver."

Samantha lifted her steaming cup. "Fuel for the final touches. I can't wait to see this beauty on display at the gallery. It's going to be a night to remember."

Samantha's smile faded, and she glanced down at her coffee cup, her fingers tracing the rim. "Actually, there's something I wanted to talk to you about."

Lila looked up from her painting, sensing the hesitation in her friend's voice. "What is it?"

"It's about Evelyn." Samantha bit her lip. "She's been acting...strange lately."

Lila set down her brush, her brow furrowing. Strange? Evelyn was always so composed, so put together. "What do you mean?"

Samantha shifted in her seat. "Just little things. She's been more distracted, canceling meetings at the last minute. And the other day, I caught her arguing with someone on the phone. She sounded upset."

A flicker of unease stirred in Lila's chest. Evelyn was more than just her mentor, she was a friend, someone who had always been there for her. The thought of something wrong with her made Lila's heart clench.

"Did you hear what it was about?" Lila asked, leaning forward.

Samantha shook her head. "No, she hung up as soon as she saw me. But it sounded serious. As her assistant, I should know what's going on with the gallery." She hesitated again. "I don't know what to make of it," Samantha admitted, her brow creased with worry. "Hopefully, I'm just overreacting."

But Lila couldn't shake the feeling that something was wrong. Evelyn's strange behavior, the secretive phone call.

"No, you're right to be concerned," Lila said, reaching out to squeeze Samantha's hand. "Evelyn's not the type to get involved in drama. Something must be going on."

Samantha nodded, looking relieved to have shared her worries. "I just hope everything's okay. The gallery means everything to Evelyn."

Lila's mind was already whirring with possibilities, her curiosity piqued. She would figure out what was troubling her friend and mentor, and hopefully try to help her fix it.

"Don't worry," Lila said, determination building in her chest. "We'll figure this out. Whatever's going on with Evelyn, we'll get to the bottom of it. Hopefully, before the show next week."

Lila's mind drifted back to the day Evelyn had invited her to be one of the featured artists at the upcoming show at the Evelyn Grey Gallery. It had been a dream come true, a validation of all the hard work and countless hours she had poured into her art.

She could still picture the pride in Evelyn's eyes as she had extended the offer, the way her elegant hands had clasped Lila's paint-stained ones. "Your work is extraordinary, Lila," Evelyn had said, her voice warm with conviction. "I want the world to see it too."

Lila turned her head away from Samantha, her gaze moving to the canvas. "Speaking of the gallery show, I can't believe it's just a week away."

Samantha nodded, her eyes sparkling with excitement. "I know! It's going to be amazing. Your paintings are going to be the talk of the town."

"I hope so," Lila said, a smile playing at the corners of her lips. She turned to face Samantha fully. "There's still so much to do though. Are all the invitations sent out?"

"Almost," Samantha replied. "I just have a few more last minute additional invitations to mail out today. And the caterers are all set for the opening night reception."

Lila breathed a sigh of relief. "Thank goodness. I don't know what Evelyn would do without you, Sam."

Her eyes drifted back to the painting before her, a swirl of vibrant colors and intricate patterns that seemed to dance across the canvas. Dark to light. It was her most ambitious work yet, a visual representation of the emotions from her divorce.

"This one's special," Lila murmured, more to herself than to Samantha.

Samantha moved closer, studying the painting with an appreciative eye. "It's stunning, Lila. The way you've captured the light, the movement ... it's like the painting is alive."

Lila felt a surge of pride at her friend's words. Lila said softly, "It represents the transformation I've gone through, the pain and the growth and the hope for the future."

Samantha squeezed Lila's shoulder, a gesture of silent support. "It's perfect. Evelyn will be so proud of you."

At the mention of her mentor's name, Lila's flicker of nervousness returned. She pushed it aside, focusing instead on the thrill of anticipation that coursed through her veins. The gallery show was her chance to prove herself, to show the world that she was more than just a small-town artist with a broken heart.

"I just hope it's enough, I want to prove to myself that I can do it."

Samantha squeezed Lila's shoulder gently. "You already have, Lila. And this show is going to prove that. Speaking of which, we should probably head over to the gallery soon to finalize the arrangements."

Lila nodded, excitement bubbling up inside her at the thought of seeing her work displayed in the prestigious Evelyn Grey Gallery as a featured artist. "You're right. Let me just straighten up here, and we can head out together."

As she cleaned her brushes and palette, Lila couldn't help but feel a sense of anticipation mixed with nerves. This show felt different, more significant somehow. It was as if she was on the cusp of something big, a turning point in her life and career.

Lila gathered the pieces that needed to be taken to the gallery, and she and Sam headed for the door.

Together, they stepped out into the sunlit streets of Willow Creek.

CHAPTER 2

The sun glinted off the gallery windows as Lila and Samantha approached. Lila carried a large canvas, her muscles stretched with the size.

Evelyn stood at the entrance, her face tight and her silver streaked hair up in a tight bun. She quickly waved them inside. "Come on in, let's get everything set up."

They stepped into the gallery, the familiar scent of fresh paint and gardenia filling Lila's nostrils. She glanced at Evelyn, noting the dark circles under her green eyes and the stiffness in her posture as she walked towards the back room. As Evelyn disappeared, Lila and Samantha carried canvases through the main room of the Evelyn Grey Gallery. The normally sedate room was a flurry of activity as staff rushed to prepare for the upcoming show.

Samantha, flashed Lila an encouraging smile. Lila carefully set down her canvas, her eyes scanning the gallery. The space was alive with activity, staff members scurrying about hanging paintings and adjusting lighting. She felt a flutter of excitement in her chest, imagining her work displayed on these walls.

"It's almost time!" Sam said.

Lila nodded, a flicker of excitement and nerves dancing in her eyes. This show represented a new chapter, a chance to rebuild after the painful unraveling of her marriage. She needed this, now more than ever.

Evelyn reemerged from the back room, her usually poised demeanor marred by visible stress. She hurried over to meet them, her smile not quite reaching her eyes.

"Lila, Samantha." Evelyn's words tumbled out in a breathless rush as she ushered them to a space deeper in the gallery. "We've got so much left to do and the opening is in just a week."

"We'll get it all set up, don't worry," Lila assured her, studying Evelyn's strained expression. Something was off, more than just pre-show jitters, but now wasn't the time to pry with still so much to do.

As they wound their way through the gallery, Lila couldn't shake the sense that Evelyn was holding something back. But Lila pushed those thoughts aside, determined to focus on the task at hand.

Lila tilted her head, studying Evelyn as she hastily sorted through a stack of papers on a table in the back. The tension in Evelyn's shoulders was palpable, her brow furrowed in concentration.

"Evelyn, is everything alright?" Lila asked gently. "You seem a bit on edge. Anything else I can help with for the show?"

Evelyn's eyes flicked up briefly before returned to what was in front of her. "No, no, everything's fine. Just a lot to get done before the opening. Have you finished unpacking those boxes yet?" Her tone was clipped, distracted.

"Almost," Lila replied, fighting back a frown. She exchanged a worried glance with Samantha, who hovered nearby, sorting through a box of glossy brochures. Something wasn't right with Evelyn. The gallery owner, who was usually composed and collected, appeared visibly tense and on edge.

Lila tried again. "Are you sure there's nothing bothering you? We've been through a lot together. You know you can talk to me, right? "

Evelyn sighed, finally meeting Lila's gaze. For a moment, a flicker of vulnerability crossed her face, but it vanished just as quickly. "I appreciate the concern, Lila, but really, I'm fine. Let's just focus on getting ready for the show, alright? There will be plenty of time to chat later."

Lila nodded slowly, unconvinced. She knew Evelyn well enough to recognize when she was holding something back. But pushing now would only make her retreat further.

As Evelyn bustled off to work on something else that needed to get done, Lila caught Samantha's eye again. A silent communication passed between them. There was definitely more going on than pre-show stress.

Lila turned back to her artwork waiting to be hung. The mystery of Evelyn's behavior would have to wait. For now, the art came first.

Lila carefully lifted a vibrant abstract painting, her eyes tracing the bold brush strokes. As she stepped toward the gallery wall, Evelyn appeared at her side, her brow furrowed.

"No, not there," Evelyn said sharply, pointing to the opposite wall. "It needs to be hung over there, where the light is more muted."

Lila paused, glancing at the spot Evelyn indicated. "Are you sure? I thought we had agreed—"

"Just do as I say, please," Evelyn interrupted, her tone clipped, her hand on her temple. She turned on her heel and strode across the room, leaving Lila standing with the painting in her hands.

Samantha caught Lila's eye from where she was arranging a series of charcoal sketches. She raised her eyebrows, silently mouthing, "What's going on?"

Lila shook her head, her own concern growing. Evelyn was never this terse, especially not when it came to curating her shows.

As Lila carefully hung the painting in its new location, the gallery door swung open, the bell above it jingling. Graham Whitaker strode in, his tailored suit and polished shoes a stark contrast to the paint-splattered blouses Lila usually wore.

The atmosphere in the room shifted instantly, a palpable tension settling over the space. Lila watched as Evelyn stiffened, her shoulders squaring as she turned to face Graham.

"What are you doing here?" Evelyn asked, her voice tight. "We are trying to prepare for a show."

Graham smirked, his eyes sweeping over the half-arranged artwork. "Just thought I'd drop by and see how things are shaping up. Though from the looks of it, Lila needs to be worried."

Lila bristled at the condescension in his tone, but confusion soon took over. Graham had wanted Lila to showcase her work at his gallery, but Lila had chosen Evelyn's gallery instead.

Evelyn took a step forward, her chin lifted. "The gallery is closed, we're in the middle of preparing for an upcoming show, which you are welcome to attend … as a guest."

"This will only take a moment," Graham retorted, running a finger along the edge of a nearby canvas. "And I must say, Evelyn, I'm surprised you're showcasing this artist. Her work is rather … derivative, don't you think?"

Lila's heart sank at his words, a flicker of doubt sparking in her chest. She glanced at Samantha, who shot her a reassuring smile before turning a glare on Graham.

As Evelyn and Graham continued their verbal sparring, their voices low but sharp, Lila couldn't shake the feeling that there was more to their animosity than a simple professional rivalry—it spoke of a deeper history.

But she had a show to help set up. Squaring her shoulders, Lila turned back to the artwork, her thoughts racing with ideas for the ideal layout. She wouldn't let Graham's snide remarks get under her skin.

Evelyn and Graham moved to a front corner of the gallery, their hushed voices carrying a hint of tension. Evelyn's face tightened as she spoke in clipped tones. "I don't appreciate you barging in here unannounced, Graham. We are getting ready for Lila's and Adrian's night."

Graham leaned in closer, his words inaudible to Lila from across the room. She strained to catch snippets of their conversation, but the low murmur of their voices was drowned out by the rustling of tissue paper as she and Samantha unwrapped the paintings.

Evelyn replied coolly. "I won't be bullied by you."

Lila, arranged a canvas nearby, was now desperate to try to overhear their conversation. She discreetly watched their body language, noticing how Evelyn stood rigidly with arms crossed while Graham loomed over her, his posture aggressive.

Graham's voice dropped to a menacing whisper. "Don't test me, Evelyn. You have no idea who you're dealing with. I always get what I want in the end."

"Is that a threat?" Evelyn arched an eyebrow, unflinching.

Lila strained to hear more, her curiosity piqued by the heated exchange. She sensed there was something more beneath the surface. This felt personal.

She watched as Evelyn leaned in closer to Graham, her words too quiet to catch. Graham scowled and shook his head vehemently. Their conversation continued, the tension thick.

Graham's voice rose above the hushed conversation, his frustration bleeding through. "I've had enough of your excuses, Evelyn. You know it's the right thing to do."

Evelyn's face remained impassive, her green eyes fixed on Graham with an icy intensity. "The decision has been made. I suggest you accept it gracefully and move on." Her words were clipped, devoid of warmth.

Lila strained to catch the details of their exchange, her concern growing because of the tension between the two gallery owners.

Samantha sidled up beside Lila, her brow furrowed with concern. She placed a gentle hand on Lila's arm, her eyes darting nervously between Graham and Evelyn. "Maybe we should give them some privacy," she whispered, her voice tinged with unease.

But Lila couldn't tear herself away, her eyes fixed on the tense exchange across the room. She was beginning to understand why Sam was so worried.

Graham took a step closer to Evelyn, his lean frame taut with barely contained anger. "You can't keep shutting me out like this. We had an agreement."

Evelyn's composure faltered for a fleeting moment, a flicker of emotion crossing her elegant features. But just as quickly, the mask slipped back into place. "I made a business decision, Graham. It's time you accepted that and focused on your own gallery."

Lila watched the exchange with rapt attention. Curiosity engulfed her as she thought about the situation.

Graham's words cut through the gallery like a knife. "You will regret this, Evelyn." His voice was low and menacing, a stark contrast to the polished veneer he usually had. The gallery had gone so quiet that everyone, had seemed to hear it

Evelyn stood tall, her green eyes flashing with a mix of anger and defiance. But she said nothing, letting the silence stretch between them like a taut wire.

Graham turned on his heel and stormed out, the glass door slamming shut behind him with finality. The sudden quiet was suffocating, broken only by the hum of traffic outside.

Lila watched as Evelyn's shoulders slumped, the bravado draining out of her mentor's frame. She wanted to go to her, but something held her back. Beside her, Samantha shifted uneasily, her hand grazing Lila's arm in a subtle gesture of support.

After a long moment, Evelyn turned to face them. A forced smile stretched across her elegant features, not quite reaching her eyes. "I apologize for the disruption everyone. Let's get back to work, shall we?"

Her tone was light, too casual, and Lila felt a prickle of unease. She knew Evelyn well enough to recognize the cracks in her composure, the tension just beneath the surface.

But Evelyn was already moving, her heels clicking against the polished floor as she strode towards the back of the gallery. Lila exchanged a glance with Sam, a silent understanding passing between them. There was definitely something going on with Evelyn.

Whatever had transpired with Graham, Lila assumed it was far from over. And as Lila turned back to the paintings, her mind raced with questions.

Lila watched Evelyn from the corner of her eye as she took another shaky breath, trying to compose herself. The uneasy silence that had settled over the gallery after Graham's abrupt departure was palpable. Unable to contain her curiosity any longer, Lila approached Evelyn, her voice gentle but probing. "Evelyn, what was that all about with Graham? It seemed like more than a minor disagreement."

Evelyn's green eyes flickered with a mix of emotions - frustration, weariness, and something else Lila couldn't quite decipher. She waved a dismissive hand. "It's nothing, dear, just a minor business disagreement that Graham and I need to sort out ourselves. Nothing for you to worry about."

Lila studied Evelyn's face, noting the tightness around her mouth and the slight furrow between her brows. There was definitely more to this than Evelyn was letting on. Evelyn's fingers fidgeted with the sleeve of her blouse, a slight hitch in her breathing.

"Are you sure?" Lila pressed gently. "It seemed pretty heated. If there's anything I can do to help ..."

"No, no," Evelyn cut her off, her voice sharp. She softened her tone immediately, offering Lila a tight smile. "I appreciate your concern, Lila, but truly, it's a small thing. Graham and I have had our fair share of disagreements like these over the years. It comes with the territory in this business. I'll get it sorted"

Lila nodded slowly, not entirely convinced but sensing Evelyn's reluctance to share more. She knew that pushing too hard would only make Evelyn retreat. Still, Lila couldn't help but be concerned.

Lila bit her lip, her unease battling her resolve to respect Evelyn's privacy. But she knew she needed to follow Evelyn's lead. She glanced at Evelyn, noticing the tightness around her eyes, the way her fingers gripped the edge of the gallery desk.

"I understand," Lila said softly, offering a reassured smile. "But, if you change your mind and there's anything I can do to help, just let me know."

Evelyn's shoulders relaxed slightly, a flicker of gratitude crossing her face. "Thank you, Lila. I appreciate your concern, but, it's nothing I can't handle." She straightened, smoothing the front of her tailored blazer. "Now, let's focus on making this show a success, shall we?"

Lila nodded, her gaze drifting to the canvases awaiting their final placements. She moved towards the nearest painting, her hands itching to adjust its position, to find the perfect balance of light and shadow.

As they worked, Lila's mind boiled over with unanswered questions. But for now, Lila pushed those thoughts aside, focusing her energy into the task at hand. She would respect Evelyn's boundaries.

CHAPTER 3

The lingering tension from Evelyn's argument with Graham dissipated. Lila's eyes scanned the room, taking in the bustling activity as artists and staff prepared for the upcoming show. Adrian Walters, the other featured artist, stood off to the side. His paint-stained hands carefully arranging a large abstract canvas. Julian Thompson hovered nearby, his critical gaze sweeping over the artwork.

Lila approached Adrian, a smile tugging at her lips. "Adrian, these are incredible."

Adrian glanced up, his intense brown eyes meeting hers. "Thanks, Lila," a hint of nervousness in his voice. "I'm still not sure about this one though." He gestured to the large abstract canvas before him, a swirl of deep blues and vibrant oranges clashing on the surface.

Lila placed a reassuring hand on his arm. "Stop second-guessing yourself. These pieces are beautiful."

Adrian's shoulders relaxed slightly at Lila's words. "You really think so? I've been stressing over this one for weeks."

Lila nodded, understanding the feeling all too well. She studied the canvas, taking in the bold strokes and vibrant colors. "I do," she said firmly. "The way you've captured the tension between warm and cool tones is incredible."

Adrian's lips quirked into a small smile. "Thanks, Lila. That means a lot coming from you." He glanced around the gallery, taking in the flurry of activity. "I can't believe the opening is just a week away. Are you nervous?"

Lila let out a soft chuckle, running a hand through her blonde hair. "Nervous? I'm absolutely terrified," she admitted. "But excited too. This show means everything."

Adrian nodded in understanding. "I know the feeling. It's like putting your heart on display."

Lila nodded in agreement, a mix of excitement and nerves fluttering in her stomach. "Exactly. It's exhilarating and terrifying all at once."

Samantha had drifted over to Julian, her quiet presence a stark contrast to his air of sophistication. "I've read some of your reviews," she said shyly. "You seem quite critical when it comes to the local art scene."

Julian adjusted his designer glasses, a hint of a smirk playing on his lips. "I simply have high standards. Too many artists in this town are content with mediocrity, churning out imitative work that lack any real depth or originality."

Samantha furrowed her brow, a flicker of disagreement in her eyes. "I'm not sure I agree, Julian. The artists in this community pour their hearts into their work. There's a raw authenticity here that you don't find in the big city art scenes."

As Julian launched into a lengthy critique, Lila's thoughts wandered away from the gossipy art critic and back to Evelyn. The gallery owner had been uncharacteristically absent since her argument with Graham, and a nagging sense of unease tugged at Lila. She expected Evelyn to be in the middle of everything; it was her gallery after all.

Julian leaned closer to Samantha to continue their conversation, his eyes narrowing as he surveyed the gallery. "Evelyn may have an eye for talent, but she's made some rather interesting enemies along the way."

His words caught Lila's attention. She turned her attention back toward Sam and Julian, her curiosity piqued. What enemies? Evelyn always seemed so well-respected in the art community.

"Oh? Do tell," Samantha prompted, her voice low and conspiratorial, loving the gossip.

A smirk played at the corners of Julian's mouth. "Let's just say not everyone appreciates her...particular brand of ruthless ambition. Artists scorned, collectors slighted. You don't get to the top without stepping on a few toes." He inspected his immaculate nails. "Or so I've heard."

Lila frowned. What Julian was saying couldn't be true. She'd known Evelyn for years. The woman he was describing did not seem like the woman that Lila looked up to as a mentor.

The back office door swung open and Evelyn strode in, her heels clicking authoritatively on the floor. Lila noted the tightness around her eyes, the rigid set of her shoulders as she and Samantha moved through the gallery to meet her.

"Lila, Samantha, thank you again for all your help," Evelyn said briskly, not quite meeting their eyes. "I have a private meeting shortly, so I'll lock up the gallery myself tonight. I trust you have everything under control here?"

"Of course, Evelyn. We're just putting the finishing touches on things," Lila assured her, studying Evelyn's face for any flicker of something. But Evelyn's expression remained carefully neutral.

Evelyn nodded. "Excellent. I knew I could count on you both." She turned on her heel. "If you'll excuse me, I need to get a few things together before my meeting."

And with that, she disappeared into her office again, the door clicking shut behind her with an air of finality. Lila stared after her, Julian's words ringing in her ears.

Lila turned to Samantha, their eyes meeting in a shared glance heavy with unspoken questions. The tension from Evelyn's strange behavior hung thick in the air, an invisible weight pressing down on them both.

Samantha bit her lip. "Is it just me, or was that..."

"Weird," Lila finished. "Definitely weird."

"Did you notice how focused Adrian was on his work? He barely looked up during the conversation between Evelyn and Graham."

Samantha nodded. "He's always been insecure, but this is a whole new level. It's like nothing else exists."

"I admire his commitment," Lila said, her thoughts drifting to her own artistic process. "But I think he is just nervous with the show so close."

"And then there's Julian," Samantha said, rolling her eyes. "He just can't help himself, can he? Always has to make those snide little comments."

Lila's brow furrowed. "He has always been a bit of a gossip. What did he say to you?"

"Oh, just his usual spiel about how the art scene here is so 'provincial' compared to New York. But then he mentioned something about Evelyn making enemies. That caught my attention."

"That part I did hear, but that doesn't sound like Evelyn at all. She's always been supportive of artists, especially up-and-coming ones."

Samantha nodded in agreement. "I know. It seems so out of character. But Julian seemed sure."

The urge to dig deeper tugged at Lila. But she hesitated. Evelyn was her friend and mentor. If she wanted to keep her personal matters private, Lila needed to respect that.

"I'm sure Evelyn can handle whatever it is," Lila said, trying to convince herself as much as Samantha. "She's always been tough."

Samantha sighed. "I hope you're right. I just hate seeing her stressed. It makes my job harder when she doesn't tell me things. How can I help if I don't know what's going on"

As they continued working, Lila couldn't shake the feeling that something big was brewing. For now, she would have to trust that Evelyn knew what she was doing. But if her friend needed her, Lila would be ready to help.

Lila caught Samantha's eye. A silent understanding passed between them, their concern for Evelyn evident. Lila's brow furrowed as she considered what she saw.

Samantha interrupted the quiet, her voice low. "Are you sure we shouldn't talk to Evelyn tonight?"

"No," Lila murmured, chewing her lip. "You know Evelyn. She plays things close to the vest. If she wanted us to know, she'd tell us."

"True. Still, I hate seeing her like this. Especially with the show so close." Samantha's eyes were clouded with worry.

"Me too." Lila sighed, glancing toward Evelyn's office door.

Something poked at Lila. But Evelyn deserved her privacy to handle whatever this was in her own way, in her own time.

"I suppose all we can do is be there for her, let her know she has our support," Lila said at last, with resignation.

Samantha nodded. "Absolutely. She's always had our backs. It's time we have hers, in whatever way she needs."

Collecting their things, Lila and Samantha made their way towards the door, the sound of their footsteps echoing through the gallery. Lila cast one last glance over her shoulder at Evelyn's closed door.

Her hand on the door, she paused, a pang of unease twisting in her gut. Something told her that whatever Evelyn was mixed up in, it was bigger than any of them realized. And sooner or later, the truth would come out - whether Evelyn was ready for it or not.

As they stepped out into the evening air, Lila couldn't shake the nagging feeling. Something big and wrong was going on beneath the surface.

"The more I think about this, I'm not sure can let this go, Sam," Lila confessed as they walked towards their cars. "Evelyn's hiding something, and I'm worried it's something serious."

Samantha shot her a sidelong glance, disbelief shown in the lines of her face at Lila's change of heart. "I know, Lila. But you said we have to trust Evelyn. She's always been private about her personal life."

Lila shook her head, her blonde waves catching the golden glow of the setting sun. "This is different. Did you see the look in her eyes? The way she practically ran to her office. That's not just privacy, that's fear. You heard the end of that argument."

They reached Lila's car, and she paused with her hand on the door handle, turning to face Samantha fully. "I can't just sit back and watch. If Evelyn's in trouble, I owe her too much not to help."

Samantha sighed, her shoulders slumping in resignation. "I understand, Lila. What are you gonna do? Don't go digging up secrets that might be dangerous."

Lila offered a tight smile, the determination burning in her blue eyes. "What would be dangerous in Willow Creek? I'll be careful. But I have to do this- for Evelyn's sake."

With that, she slid into her car, her mind already racing with the possibilities. As she pulled out of the parking lot, Lila knew one thing - she wouldn't rest until she uncovered the truth behind Evelyn's strange behavior. Lila would find the answers.

Chapter 4

The morning sunlight glinted off the glass doors of the Evelyn Grey Gallery as Lila and Samantha approached, their hands full of more supplies and decorations for the upcoming show. Lila's blond waves were pulled back in a messy bun, and her paint-splattered shirt fluttered in the breeze.

"I can't believe the show is only a week away," Lila said, her blue eyes sparkling with excitement. "Evelyn is going to be thrilled with how everything comes together."

Samantha nodded, adjusting her grip on a large vase of flowers. "She's put so much work into this show." She stopped at the gallery entrance to unlock the door.

Samantha reached with her keys, expecting to feel the familiar resistance of the lock. To her surprise, the handle turned easily and the door swung open slightly.

She paused, her brow furrowing in confusion, as she peered into the gallery

"That's strange," she muttered.

Lila followed her gaze and felt a flicker of unease. Evelyn was always meticulous about security, ensuring the gallery was locked tight each night. An unlocked door was unheard of.

Sam's brow furrowed. "Do you think she forgot?"

Lila shook her head, a sense of foreboding settling in her gut. "No, not Evelyn. She probably beat us here this morning" She reached out and pushed the door open more, the hinges creaking softly.

As they stepped inside, an eerie stillness enveloped them. The gallery felt cold and empty, the silence broken only by the echo of their footsteps on the polished floor. Lila's heart raced as she scanned the room, searching for any sign of Evelyn.

"Evelyn?" Lila called out, her voice sounding small in the vast space. "Are you here?"

Lila and Samantha stepped cautiously into the gallery, their footsteps echoing through the empty space. The usual bustling energy of the gallery was replaced by an eerie stillness that sent shivers down their spines.

"Evelyn?" Lila called out, her voice echoing back, ss she put her box down on the floor.

Samantha's voice joined hers, a note of worry creeping in as she gripped the vase tighter. "Evelyn, are you here? It's Lila and Sam."

Their words bounced off the walls, reverberating through the empty gallery, but no response came. Lila's mind raced with possibilities, each more unsettling than the last. She glanced at Samantha, seeing her own concern mirrored in her friend's eyes.

"Maybe she's in her office," Samantha suggested, her voice hushed as if afraid to disturb the quiet.

Lila nodded, a knot forming in her stomach as they moved deeper into the gallery. The familiar artwork lining the walls seemed to take on a sinister aspect in the dim light, the once-vibrant colors now muted and gloomy.

As they approached Evelyn's office, Lila's steps faltered. The door stood slightly ajar, a sliver of darkness visible beyond. A cold dread settled over her, a sense that something was terribly wrong.

"Evelyn?" Lila called again, her voice trembling slightly. "Are you there?"

Silence greeted them, broken only by the beating of their hearts. Lila reached out, her hand shaking as she pushed the door open wider. The hinges creaked, the sound cutting through the stillness like a knife.

Lila's breath caught in her throat as she took in the sight before her. Evelyn's office was in disarray, papers strewn across the floor, furniture overturned. And there, in the center of the chaos, lay Evelyn', a dark pool of blood beneath her.

A scream tore from Samantha's throat as she dropped the vase, shattering the silence. Lila stood frozen, her mind struggling to process the scene before her. But the metallic scent of blood and the chill in the air told her otherwise.

Lila's mind reeled as she stared at Evelyn's lifeless form, unable to tear her gaze away.

"We need to call the police," Lila managed to whispered, her voice barely audible. She fumbled for her phone, her fingers numb and clumsy as she dialed the emergency number.

Samantha nodded, her face pale and streaked with tears. She reached out, grasping Lila's free hand, seeking comfort in the shared horror of the moment.

As the phone rang, Lila's thoughts raced. Lila's hand trembled as she held the phone to her ear, her eyes fixed on Evelyn's still form. Why would anyone want to hurt Evelyn?

The operator's voice crackled through the phone, jolting Lila back to reality. She struggled to find the words, her voice shaking as she relayed the terrible news.

"Please, send help," she pleaded. "There's been a murder at the Evelyn Grey Gallery."

The words felt foreign on her tongue, as if she were speaking about someone else's life, someone else's tragedy. But as she ended the call and turned back to Samantha, the weight of the situation crashed over her.

Lila's legs gave way, and she sank to the floor, her back pressed against the wall. Samantha joined her, their shoulders touching as they huddled together, trying to make sense of the situation.

"I can't believe this is happening," Samantha whispered, her voice raw with emotion. "Who would do something like this?"

Lila shook her head, unable to find an answer. Her mind swirled with questions, with fears, with a growing sense of anger and determination.

As the distant wail of sirens grew louder, Lila and Samantha clung to each other, together in their grief. Lila's mind raced as she stared at Evelyn's lifeless form, unable to tear her gaze away. The metallic scent of blood filled the air, making her stomach churn. She forced herself to take deep breaths, trying to calm the panic rising in her chest.

The gallery that was once peaceful had transformed into a crime scene. The flashing red and blue lights of the police cars cast an eerie glow through the windows.

Lila and Samantha watched from a bench in the middle of the gallery as uniformed officers swarmed the building, their movement through the halls like a tornado. The low murmur of voices, the crackle of radios, and the occasional sounds from equipment invaded the space.

"I can't believe this is happening," Samantha repeated, her voice barely above a whisper. "It feels like a nightmare."

Lila nodded, her eyes fixed on the doorway to Evelyn's office. She half-expected Evelyn to emerge at any moment, her vibrant smile lighting up the room as she welcomed them. But the door remained closed.

"We should have been here earlier," Samantha said, her voice heavy with guilt. "Maybe if we had…"

"Don't," Lila interrupted, her hand finding Samantha's and squeezing it tightly. "Don't do that to yourself. This isn't your fault."

Samantha knew Lila was right, but the weight of responsibility still pressed down on her shoulders. Evelyn had been more than just a mentor; she had been a friend. The idea of never seeing her again was almost unbearable.

As they sat there, watching the controlled chaos unfold around them, Lila's mind drifted to an earlier conversation she had with Evelyn. They had discussed the upcoming gallery show, the excitement in Evelyn's voice palpable. Lila had promised to be there early, to help with the final preparations.

The promise she had kept, but it didn't seem to matter anymore.

The guilt twisted in her gut like a knife. She should have been there. Maybe she could have done something to help.

"Lila Montgomery, Samantha Erikson?" a deep voice interrupted her thoughts.

Lila looked up to see a tall, broad-shouldered man standing before her. He wore a tailored suit that spoke of authority, and his blue eyes seemed to see straight through her.

"I'm Detective Marcus Reed," he introduced himself, flashing a badge. "I understand you were the ones who discovered the body?"

Lila nodded, her throat suddenly dry. She swallowed hard, forcing herself to meet the detective's gaze.

"Yes," she replied, her voice barely above a whisper. "We... we found her like that. In her office."

Detective Reed nodded, his expression unreadable. He pulled out a small notebook and pen, his eyes never leaving Lila's face.

"I know this is difficult," he said, his tone softening slightly. "But I need you to tell me everything you remember. Every detail, no matter how small."

Lila took a deep breath, steeling herself for the painful recollection. As she and Samantha prepared to recount the events of the morning, her voice shook with emotion, but she pushed through, determined to provide whatever information she could to help catch Evelyn's killer.

Lila stepped forward, her eyes glistening with unshed tears. "We arrived at the gallery early this morning," she began, her voice steady. "The door was unlocked, which was unusual. Evelyn always made sure everything was secure."

Detective Reed jotted down notes, his pen moving swiftly across the page. "And then what happened? Did you notice anything else unusual when you arrived?" he asked, his eyes scanning the two women's faces.

Lila thought back to their arrival that morning. Everything seemed normal, just as it always did at the gallery.

"No," she replied truthfully. "Everything looked the same as it always does."

Detective Reed jotted down some more notes before turning to Samantha. "And you, Ms. Erikson? Did you notice anything out of place?"

Samantha shook her head, her eyes still wet with tears. "No, nothing. The office door was cracked," Samantha whispered, a single tear escaping down her cheek. "We pushed it open wider and ... and that's when we saw her."

Lila closed her eyes, the image of Evelyn's lifeless body seared into her mind. The pool of blood, the unnatural stillness, the sheer wrongness of it all.

Detective Reed's voice cut through the painful memories. "Did you notice anything out of place? Any signs of a struggle or forced entry?"

Lila shook her head, trying to clear the fog of grief and shock. "Well, the office was a mess; it's usually pretty organized. Our focus went straight to Evelyn, who was on the floor."

The detective nodded, his expression thoughtful. "And after you discovered the body, what did you do?"

"We called 911," Samantha replied, her voice a little steadier now. "And then we waited. We didn't touch anything, we just... we couldn't believe it was real."

Lila met Detective Reed's gaze, her own eyes burning with a fierce determination. "Detective, Evelyn was more than just a colleague. She was a friend, a mentor. She didn't deserve this."

The detective's stoic expression softened slightly, a flicker of understanding in his eyes. "I promise you, we will do everything in our power to find out what happened and bring that person to justice."

As the detective turned to confer with his team, Lila felt a surge of gratitude mixed with the overwhelming grief.

Detective Reed moved methodically through Evelyn's office, his keen eyes scanning every detail. He crouched beside the body, careful not to disturb anything as he examined the position of the body and the surrounding evidence. His gloved hands gently lifted a strand of hair from Evelyn's face, his expression grim.

"Bag and tag everything," he instructed his team, his voice cutting through the heavy silence. "I want photos of every angle and every piece of evidence documented."

As the crime scene technicians moved in, their cameras flashing and equipment whirring, Lila felt a growing sense of unease. The once vibrant gallery now felt contaminated.

Detective Reed approached them again, his expression carefully neutral. "I know this is difficult, but I need to ask you a few more questions."

Lila nodded, steeling herself. "Of course, Detective. Anything to help find who did this."

"Did Evelyn have any enemies? Anyone who might have held a grudge against her?"

Samantha shook her head. "No, everyone loved Evelyn. She was always so supportive, so generous with her time and advice."

Lila frowned, "Well..." she began hesitantly, "there was something Julian Thompson said yesterday that seemed odd at the time."

Detective Reed's eyebrows raised slightly. "Julian Thompson? The art critic?"

Lila nodded, her brow furrowing as she recalled Julian's words from the day before. "Yes, Julian was at the gallery yesterday. He's always been a bit of a gossip, but something he said stood out."

Detective Reed leaned in, his interest piqued.

Lila took a deep breath, her mind racing back to the previous day. "Julian mentioned that Evelyn had 'made some interesting enemies along the way.' He said something about her 'ruthless ambition' and how she'd 'stepped on toes' to get to the top."

Detective Reed made a note in his pad. "Do you have any idea who he was talking about? I'll need a name and any contact information you have."

"I'm sorry, I don't know who he was talking about" Lila replied. "Also..."

"What?"

Lila took a deep breath, her mind racing back to the previous day. "There was also an incident with Graham Whitaker yesterday," she began, her voice low but steady. "He's the owner of a another gallery across town."

Detective Reed's eyebrows raised slightly. "Go on?"

Lila's brow furrowed as she recalled the tense exchange between Evelyn and Graham. "Graham stormed into the gallery yesterday, completely unannounced. He and Evelyn got into a heated argument. I couldn't hear any details, but it was clear there was something going on,"

The detective's radio crackled to life, and he excused himself to take the call. Lila turned to Samantha, her eyes filled with a fierce determination.

Lila's gaze drifted across the gallery, taking in the controlled chaos of the crime scene. Officers moved with purpose, their hushed conversations punctuated by the occasional crackle of police radios. The once vibrant space now felt somber and hollow, a stark contrast to the lively atmosphere that had filled it just days before.

Detective Reed returned, his expression grim. "We've got a team canvassing the area for potential witnesses. In the meantime, I'll need you both to come down to the station for formal statements."

Samantha's eyes widened. "You don't think... you don't suspect us, do you?"

"It's standard procedure," Marcus assured her. "We need to gather all the information we can, and your statements will help us build a timeline of events."

Lila nodded, her voice steady despite the tumult of emotions within her. "Of course, Detective. We'll do whatever we can to help."

"Good," said Detective Marcus. "I'll can get someone to drive you there in a few minutes, if you need. But I won't be there for a few hours. I need to finish up here."

"If you don't mind, can we wait here?"

"Not inside. If you want to wait outside the gallery till I finish, you can."

Lila nodded and turned her and Samantha around and toward the exit of the gallery. She was lost in her memories of Evelyn.

"Lila?" Samantha's touch on her arm pulled her from her thoughts. "Are you okay?"

"I will be," Lila replied, her jaw set with determination. "Once we know who did this."

Lila and Samantha stepped outside and away from the chaos of the crime scene. The flashing lights of the police cars cast an eerie glow across the gallery's façade.

Samantha's hand found Lila's, their fingers intertwining in a silent gesture of support. "What do we do now?" Her voice barely audible above the chaos of the investigation.

Lila's gaze remained fixed on the gallery entrance, where officers moved in and out. "We let the police do their job," she repeated, her tone laced with a quiet determination.

As they watched the police work, Lila's mind raced with possibilities. Who would want to harm Evelyn? What enemies had Julian been talking about? The questions piled up, each one adding to the growing sense of unease that settled in the pit of her stomach.

Detective Reed finally emerged from the gallery, his face etched with the weight of the case. He approached Lila and Samantha, his notepad in hand. "I think the formal statements can wait till tomorrow. Can you meet me at the station in the morning?" He said. "I know this isn't easy. In the meantime, go home."

Lila nodded, a lump forming in her throat. Lila and Samantha exchanged a glance, both reluctant to leave the scene despite Detective Reed's suggestion. The thought of going home, of trying to carry on with normal life while Evelyn's killer remained at large, felt impossible.

"Actually, Detective, if it's alright with you, we'd like to stay here a bit longer. It just doesn't feel right to leave yet."

Detective Reed studied them for a moment, his expression softening slightly. "I understand," he said with a nod. "You can stay, but please remain outside the police line. And if you remember anything else, anything at all, don't hesitate to contact me."

The detective turned back towards the gallery.

CHAPTER 5

Lila stood beside Samantha on the sidewalk, her eyes fixed on the gallery's entrance. The cloudy morning light cast a somber Grey over the scene. A growing crowd of onlookers huddled nearby, their hushed murmurs mingling with the distant wail of sirens.

Lila replayed the horrific discovery in her mind—Evelyn's lifeless body sprawled on the gallery floor, the colorful artwork adorning the walls provided a striking contrast to the morbid scene. She shivered, wrapping her arms tightly around herself. Beside her, Samantha shifted from foot to foot, her normally bright eyes clouded with grief and confusion.

"I can't believe she's gone," Samantha whispered, her voice cracking. "Evelyn lived for this gallery. It was her pride and joy."

Lila nodded, swallowing the lump in her throat. "Remember how excited she was for this show? She poured all her energy into making it perfect."

Sam's frown deepened as she tucked a stray lock of hair behind her ear. "This really puts things into perspective," she said, her voice filled with tension. "I thought it was just the stress of the show she was worried about, but now..." She trailed off, her brow furrowed in concern.

Lila's mind raced with the same question as before. Who would want to hurt Evelyn? Why would anyone have had a reason to harm her?

A sudden movement caught Lila's eye. In the distance, a woman approached, her pace brisk and purposeful. Even from afar, Lila could see the mix of confusion and shock etched on her face. The woman's colorful short cropped hair stood out against her pale skin.

"Who's that?" Samantha murmured, following Lila's gaze.

Lila shook her head. "I don't know, but she seems to be heading straight for the gallery."

They watched as the woman drew closer, her steps faltering as she neared the police tape cordoning off the entrance. A gasp escaped her lips, and she stood frozen, visibly disturbed by the scene before her.

"What's going on here?" the woman demanded, her voice carrying across the murmuring crowd. "I have an appointment with Evelyn Grey. Where is she?"

Lila and Samantha exchanged curious glances. The woman's words hung in the air, raising more questions than answers.

The woman turned to face the onlookers, her eyes wide and desperate. "My name is Maxine Banks. Evelyn and I were supposed to meet today," she repeated, her voice rising with panic. "Can someone please tell me what's happened?"

Lila felt a chill run down her spine. She stepped forward, drawing Maxine's attention. "Ms. Banks," her voice gentle but firm, "I'm afraid I have some bad news. Evelyn..." She paused, struggling to find the right words. "Evelyn was found dead this morning."

Maxine's face drained of color, her eyes widening in shock. Her legs seemed to give out beneath her, and she stumbled backwards, nearly collapsing onto the sidewalk. Lila rushed forward, catching the woman's arm to steady her.

"Dead?" Maxine whispered, her voice barely audible. "No, that can't be right. We were supposed to talk about a possible upcoming show today." Maxine's eyes darted frantically between Lila and the gallery entrance, as if hoped to see Evelyn emerge at any moment.

Samantha stepped closer, her voice soft with sympathy. "I'm so sorry. We're all in shock too. Did you know Evelyn well?"

Maxine's eyes glistened with unshed tears. "I've known Evelyn for years. I'm an artist, and we'd lost touch for a while when I moved to New York," she said, her voice barely above a whisper. "Life, you know?"

Maxine's gaze lingered on the gallery entrance for a moment longer before she abruptly turned away, her shoulders hunched and her steps unsteady. Lila watched as the woman made her way through the crowd, her vibrant hair a beacon amidst the sea of somber faces. The artist approached an older gentleman standing near the edge of the crowd.

Samantha leaned closer to Lila, her voice low. "I've never seen her before. Do you think she's telling the truth about her appointment with Evelyn? I had no idea that Evelyn was considering another show, and I don't remember any appointments on her calendar for this morning."

Lila pursed her lips, considering the possibilities. "I'm not sure. But the timing of her arrival, just after Evelyn's death... it seems odd, don't you think?"

As they watched Maxine, Lila couldn't shake the feeling that there was more to her story than she was letting on.

Detective Marcus Reed came out of the gallery and approached Maxine, his steps measured and his expression composed. "Ms. Banks, I'm Detective Reed. I understand this must be a shock, but I need you to take a deep breath and try to stay calm."

Maxine's eyes darted to the detective, her hands trembling slightly. "Detective, please, what happened to Evelyn? We were supposed to meet today. I... I can't believe this is happening."

Detective Reed raised his hands slightly to try and calm Maxine down. "I know you have questions, and I promise we'll do our best to find answers. Can you tell me a little more about your relationship with Evelyn? You mentioned you knew each other?"

Maxine nodded, her gaze distant. "We did, yes. Evelyn was my mentor, my friend. But we had a falling out, over personal matters. It was just a misunderstanding, really."

Maxine took a deep breath, her eyes softening as she recalled memories of her friend. "But we got past it," she continued, her voice growing stronger. "About a month ago, Evelyn reached out to me. She said she'd seen my latest work at a small gallery in the city and was impressed. She wanted to discuss the possibility of featuring my pieces in one of her upcoming shows."

Detective Reed nodded, jotting notes in a small pad. "And that's why you were meeting today?"

"Yes," Maxine replied, her voice wavering. "We were going to discuss possible dates."

Lila and Samantha exchanged a glance, their suspicions growing with each word Maxine spoke. Lila couldn't help but wonder what kind of personal matters could have caused such a rift between Evelyn and Maxine.

As Detective Reed led Maxine to a quieter area, explaining the need for a formal statement, Lila's mind raced with questions. The vagueness of Maxine's story, the convenient timing of her arrival - it all seemed too coincidental to be mere chance.

Samantha's voice pulled Lila from her thoughts. "There's something off about her, Lila. The way she talks about her past with Evelyn, it's like she's holding back. And I have never heard of her, or any other upcoming show"

Lila nodded, her eyes never leaving Maxine's retreating form. "I agree. And the fact that she shows up now, after all this time? It doesn't add up."

As Lila watched Maxine disappear into the gallery with the detective, she couldn't shake the feeling that Maxine knew more than she was saying. Her gut instinct told her that this mysterious artist was somehow connected to Evelyn's death.

Lila's gaze lingered on the spot where Maxine and Detective Reed had disappeared from view, her mind churning with unanswered questions. She turned to Samantha, her brows knitted together in thought. "I can't shake the feeling that there's more to this story than Maxine's letting on."

Samantha nodded, her eyes filled with concern. "I know what you mean. The way she talked about her falling out with Evelyn, it seemed like she was holding something back. And the timing of her arrival... it's just too perfect."

"Exactly." Lila's voice was tinged with frustration. "Evelyn had been hinting at some kind of trouble lately, but she never went into detail. I wonder if it had anything to do with Maxine."

Samantha sighed, her shoulders slumping. "I wish we had pressed Evelyn more when we had the chance. Maybe we could have helped her, or at least understood what was going on."

Lila reached out and squeezed Samantha's hand, offering a small smile of reassurance. "We couldn't have known, Sam."

Lila's instincts told her that there was a connection, some piece of information that they were missing that would tie everything together. But as much as she wanted to chase after Maxine and demand answers, she knew she had to be smart about this. The police were involved now, and the last thing she wanted was to interfere with their investigation.

"We should get some rest," Lila said. "Let's go tell Detective Reed that we are leaving and that we will be at the police station tomorrow morning to make our formal statements."

Samantha nodded, a flicker of determination in her eyes. "You're right. We'll let the police do their job. For Evelyn's sake."

As they made their way back towards the gallery, Lila couldn't shake the feeling that this was just the beginning.

CHAPTER 6

Lila drummed her fingers on the weathered diner table, her brow furrowed. "It's been a week, Sam. A week since we gave our statements and the police are no closer to finding Evelyn's killer."

Samantha sighed, stirring her coffee. "I know, Lila. But these things take time. Detective Reed is doing everything he can."

"Is he though?" Lila leaned forward, her blue eyes flashing. "Because from where I'm sitting, it doesn't seem like progress is being made at all."

Samantha reached across the table, placing a comforted hand on Lila's arm. "You can't think like that. Detective Reed is a professional. He'll find the killer."

Lila pulled away, shaking her head. "But what if he doesn't? What if the trail goes cold and Evelyn's killer is never brought to justice?" Lila's voice trembled with emotion. "I can't just sit here and do nothing."

Samantha shook her head, not liking the direction Lila was taking, her eyes widening with concern. "Lila, what are you thinking? You can't seriously be considering investigating this yourself."

Lila met her friend's gaze, a spark of determination in her blue eyes. "Why not? We knew Evelyn better than anyone. We might notice things the police would miss."

Samantha leaned back, her expression a mix of concern and exasperation. "Lila, this isn't one of your mystery novels. This is real life."

Lila's jaw tightened. She couldn't just sit idly by while Evelyn's killer walked free. She met Samantha's gaze, her voice low but resolute. "I'm going to investigate on my own. I have to find out who did this to Evelyn."

Samantha's eyes widened. "Lila, it's too dangerous."

"I can't just do nothing, Sam. I owe it to Evelyn to find the truth." Lila's hands clenched into fists, her nails digging into her palms.

"But you're not a detective. What if you get hurt? Or worse?" Samantha reached for her water to take a sip.

Lila gave her a small, grateful smile. "I appreciate your concern, but I have to do this. For Evelyn. For myself." She took a deep breath, her mind already racing with possibilities. "I'll start by retracing Evelyn's steps leading up to that night. There has to be something the police overlooked."

Samantha leaned back, studying her friend's determined expression. She knew there was no talking Lila out of this. "Just promise me you'll be careful. And keep me in the loop, okay?"

Lila nodded and her gaze drifted, her eyes clouding with a mix of frustration and sadness. "And as if losing Evelyn wasn't enough, the gallery's closed. My art show, the one I've been prepping for months, is postponed, potentially cancelled." She let out a heavy sigh, her shoulders slumping. "It feels like everything's falling apart."

Samantha reached out, giving Lila's hand a comforting squeeze. "I'm so sorry, Lila. I know how much that show meant to you, and to Evelyn."

Lila nodded, swallowing the lump in her throat. "She was so excited about it. She kept saying it was going to be my big break." A wistful smile tugged at her lips, memories of Evelyn's unwavering support flooding her mind.

The bell above the diner door chimed, drawing their attention. In strode Maxine Banks, her vibrant hair and confident demeanor commanding the room. Her eyes, sharp and curious, scanned the booths as she made her way to the counter.

Lila's brows furrowed, recognizing Maxine. "I wonder what she's still doing here."

Samantha's eyes narrowed as she watched Maxine. "I don't trust her," she muttered, her voice low and tense. "There's something off about her story."

Lila nodded, considering Maxine's profile.

Maxine settled onto a stool not far from where Lila and Sam were seated, her gaze still wandering the diner. When her eyes met Lila's, a flicker of recognition crossed her face. She turned her head back, then moved to completely face the counter. Lila's heart quickened, unsure what to make of Maxine's presence. She turned back to Samantha.

Maxine leaned forward on the counter, but her posture was stiff and attentive.

Samantha's eyes darted between Lila and Maxine, her brow furrowed with concern as she returned to their conversation. "Lila, I know you want answers, but we need to be careful. This isn't our job. We're not detectives."

Lila's hands fidgeted with her napkin, her frustration mounting. "I can't just sit back and do nothing, Sam."

"But at what cost?" Samantha's voice was gentle but firm, trying to talk her friend out of her investigation. "You're not trained for this, Lila. " Her eyes widened, the gravity of the situation sinking in. "What if you become a target?"

Lila's heart raced at the thought, but her determination didn't waver. "I can't let fear stop me from doing what's right. Evelyn deserves justice."

"I understand, but you need to think this through. Detective Reed is on the case. Let him handle it."

Lila shook her head. "He's got his hands full. He probably has a dozen other cases and can't give this case the attention it needs." She glanced over at Maxine who quickly averted her gaze, pretending to study the menu.

"I'm sure that's not true. Evelyn's death is probably his top priority right now, nothing ever happens in Willow Creek."

"Besides, I have a feeling there's more to this than meets the eye."

Samantha followed Lila's gaze, her own suspicion growing. "What are you thinking?"

"I'm not sure yet," Lila admitted, her mind racing with possibilities. "But I'm going to find out."

As if on cue, Maxine rose from her seat at the counter and approached their booth, turning heads as she moved closer. Her eyes fixed on Lila and Samantha.

Lila watched her approach. Samantha tensed, her eyes narrowing as she studied Maxine's every move. "What do you think she wants?" she whispered, her voice low and cautious.

Lila shook her head, unable to tear her gaze away from Maxine's approaching figure. "I don't know, but I have a feeling we're about to find out."

"Excuse me," Maxine said, her voice smooth and cultured. "I couldn't help but notice you two. You were at the gallery last week, weren't you?" Her gaze flickered between Lila and Samantha.

Lila and Samantha exchanged a wary glance before Lila responded, "Yes, we were. I'm Lila and this is Samantha. We were friends of Evelyn."

Maxine nodded, her expression softening slightly. "I'm Maxine Banks. I was supposed to meet with Evelyn that day." She paused, her eyes clouding with emotion. "I still can't believe she's gone."

Lila studied Maxine's face, searching for any hint of deception. "I'm sorry for your loss," she said carefully. "You mentioned you and Evelyn were friends?"

Maxine nodded, her gaze drifting to the window. "We were. We lost touch and just recently reconnected."

Lila and Samantha exchanged a cautious glance.

"Mind if I join you?" Maxine asked, her voice smooth and confident.

Lila hesitated, glancing at Samantha, who gave a slight shrug. "Not at all, please," Lila said, gesturing to the empty seat beside her. "What brings you over here?"

Maxine slid into the booth, her movements graceful and deliberate. "I couldn't help but overhear your conversation," she said, leaning forward conspiratorially. "And I think I might be able to help."

Samantha, ever the skeptic, narrowed her eyes. "Help how, exactly?"

Lila took a deep breath, weighing her options. Maxine's offer was tempting, but she couldn't ignore the nagging feeling in the pit of her stomach. She looked at Samantha, who sat rigid in her seat, her lips pressed into a thin line.

"We appreciate your offer, Maxine," Lila began, choosing her words carefully. "But we don't know you; or anything about your relationship with Evelyn."

Maxine leaned in closer, her voice dropping to a whisper. "I understand your hesitation. But I have information about Evelyn that the police don't know. Information that could help solve her murder."

Lila's heart raced at Maxine's words. She exchanged a quick glance with Samantha, whose expression was a mix of intrigue and skepticism.

"Why didn't you give this information to the police?" Sam questioned

"What kind of information?" Lila asked cautiously, leaning in closer.

Maxine glanced around the diner, her eyes darting to check if anyone was listening. Satisfied they weren't being overheard, she leaned in even closer.

"Evelyn was scared about something," Maxine whispered to Lila ignoring Sam, her voice barely audible. "She called me a few weeks ago for help with something. But she refused to give me any details over the phone."

"Why would Evelyn go to you, and not us?" Sam asked, her voice rising.

Lila placed a gentle hand on Samantha's arm, a silent plea for calm. She turned back to Maxine, her voice steady. "Samantha's right."

Maxine's eyes flickered between Lila and Samantha, a hint of uncertainty crossing her face. "I understand your skepticism," she said softly. "But Evelyn and I... we had a complicated history. There were things she felt she could share only with me."

Lila leaned forward, her curiosity piqued despite her reservations. "What kind of complicated history?"

Maxine leaned back, her eyes flickering between the two women. "It's not something I'm ready to talk about with someone I just met," she said, a hint of respect creeping into her voice. "But you're going to need all the help you can get if you want to catch Evelyn's killer. I want to help."

"Before I say yes," Lila said, turning back to Maxine. "What exactly did you have in mind?"

Maxine's smile widened, a glint of excitement in her eyes. "First things first," she said, leaning forward conspiratorially. "We need to compare notes. What do you know so far?"

Lila hesitated, her mind racing through the scant details they'd managed to uncover. She looked at

Samantha, who gave her a small shrug, as if to said, "It's up to you."

Taking a deep breath, Lila began to share what the knew so far about possible suspects, her voice low and urgent.

"First, the day before Evelyn was killed, we overheard her having a heated discussion with Graham Whittaker. It was in the middle of setting up for the art show, in full view of everyone."

Maxine nodded, her brow furrowing as she processed the information. "Graham Whittaker, the owner of the other art gallery? I've heard he can be a real piece of work."

Lila nodded, her voice dropping to a whisper. "We couldn't hear everything, but it sounded like Graham was threatening Evelyn. Something about him always getting what he wants."

Maxine leaned back, her eyes calculating. "Interesting. Sounds like motive to me."

Samantha's voice cut through the tension. "You're jumping to dangerous conclusions about Graham," she interjected. "We don't know what the argument was about."

"True," said Lila.

Samantha continued, her voice hesitant but determined. "There's also Julian Thompson, the art critic. He made a comment that same day at the gallery about the 'enemies' Evelyn had made over the years."

Lila's eyes widened, realization dawning. "That's right. I remember Julian saying that Evelyn had stepped on a lot of toes to get where she was. He was helping Adrian set up, wasn't he?"

"He was." Samantha replied.

Maxine sat back, her eyes distant as she processed the information. "Wow," she murmured, almost to herself. "All this certainly gives us a starting point."

Lila leaned forward, her heart pounding in her chest. "Do you know something we don't?"

"I'm not sure at the moment, but Evelyn is the one that called me to talk. That just seems like a strange coincidence to me."

Lila studied Maxine's face, searching for any hint of deception. Her eyes were clouded with emotion, but there was something else there too - determination.

"Alright," Lila said finally, her voice firm. "If we're going to do this, we need to be smart about it. No rash decisions, no unnecessary risks. We investigate carefully and quietly."

Maxine nodded, a glimmer of hope starting in her voice. "Agreed. Where do you think we should start?"

"I think we should start by talking to Graham, and then Adrian," Lila said decisively.

"Graham seems like the most logical place to start," Maxine said, her voice low and determined. "That argument with Evelyn the day before her death is too suspicious to ignore. But, why Adrian instead of Julian?"

Samantha nodded reluctantly. "I agree, but we need to be careful. Graham has a reputation for being ruthless."

"Then I think Adrian is a better choice than Julian. He tends to be a bit more sincere. He might know what Julian meant by enemies." Lila said

"I can go with you to talk to them if you want," Maxine said, her voice filled with conviction. "And, I have connections in the art world, people who might know things about Evelyn's past and be willing to share. Maybe I can shed some light on these 'enemies.'"

Lila felt a surge of hope. Perhaps Maxine was what they needed to help discover the truth behind Evelyn's murder. But Samantha's words of caution echoed in her mind - they needed to be careful.

"We appreciate your help, Maxine," Lila said, choosing her words carefully. "But we need to be smart about this. We can ask our own questions, but can't interfere with the official investigation either."

Maxine waved a dismissive hand. "Of course not." She leaned back, a glint of excitement in her eyes.

"We need to start by finding out more about Graham's and Julian's movements on the night of the murder," Lila said, her determination growing. "See if anyone saw them near the gallery."

Samantha sighed, her hesitation palpable. "I still think we should be careful. We don't want to tip anyone off or put ourselves in danger."

Lila reached out, grasping Samantha's hand. "I know it's risky, but I can't just sit back and do nothing. I'm going to talk to Graham, see if I can find out more about what they were arguing about."

Maxine's gaze darted between them. "We'll be careful," she assured Samantha.

Lila felt a surge of gratitude for Maxine's support. Lila turned to Maxine, her voice low and urgent. "Thank you for your help, Maxine. I really appreciate it."

Maxine leaned forward, her eyes glinting with a mix of determination and trouble. "Don't thank me yet.

We've got a lot of work to do if we're going to catch Evelyn's killer."

Lila nodded, a newfound sense of purpose filling her. With Maxine's help, they might actually have a chance at uncovering the truth. She glanced at her watch, realizing how much time had passed.

"With everything figured out, I should get going," Lila said, gathering her things. "I'll stop by Graham's gallery tomorrow, see if I can find out more about their argument. Then I'll visit Adrian the next day"

Maxine nodded, rising from her seat. "Sounds good. I have something I have to do tomorrow already, but I can go with you to Adrian's. In the mean time. I'll reach out to my contacts, see if anyone knows anything that might help."

Samantha and Lila stood as well, Sam's brows creased with lingering concern. "Just... be careful, okay? Both of you." Her gaze darted between Lila and Maxine, a silent plea in her eyes.

Lila offered her a reassuring smile. "We will." Lila gave Samantha a quick hug before they parted ways. Lila knew this would be difficult for her timid best friend. "I'll call you tomorrow after I talk to Graham, okay?"

Samantha nodded, her eyes still filled with worry. "Alright. But promise me you'll be careful. Don't push him too hard."

"I won't, you have nothing to worry about." Lila reassured.

CHAPTER 7

Lila stepped into Graham's gallery, her shoes echoing against the polished concrete floor. The spacious loft was a mixture of vibrant artwork vying for attention. Amidst the riot of color, she spotted Graham standing near a massive canvas, his chiseled features etched with a guarded expression. His arms were crossed defensively, as if bracing himself for an impending storm.

Graham's piercing blue eyes locked onto Lila as she approached, his posture stiffening imperceptibly. Lila met his gaze unflinchingly, determination glinting in her own eyes. She stopped a few feet away, her bohemian skirt swishing around her legs, as she fixed him with a penetrating stare.

"Graham," Lila said evenly, "we need to talk. I need to ask you a few questions."

"Lila," Graham replied, his tone measured. "What brings you here?"

"I know about the argument you had with Evelyn, the day before she was killed."

Graham's eyes narrowed almost imperceptibly. Lila could see the gears turning behind his carefully constructed façade, weighing his options, calculating his next move. But she refused to back down, her stance unwavering.

"I'm not sure what you're referring to," Graham said carefully, as he turned to face another painting.

"Cut the act, Graham. I know you and Evelyn had an argument. It was in full view of everyone at Evelyn's gallery." Lila followed him.

Lila watched as Graham's jaw tightened, a muscle twitching beneath the sculpted plane of his cheek. His hesitation spoke volumes. She could practically feel the tension radiating off him, see the wariness in his eyes as he contemplated his response.

"Evelyn and I had a disagreement," Graham finally said, his words measured. "But I fail to see how that's any of your concern."

"It became my concern when Evelyn turned up dead," Lila countered, her voice sharp as a knife's edge.

Graham schooled his features into a mask of cool composure and looked Lila in the eye. "I already spoke with the police about the conversation that Evelyn and

I had the day before she died. Why exactly do you need to know too?"

"I just need to know what happened between you two, Graham." Lila pleaded, "she was my friend. I just want the truth."

Graham's defensive stance softened slightly as he realized Lila wouldn't back down. He ran a hand through his hair. With a heavy sigh, he gestured towards a nearby leather sofa.

"Fine. Let's talk."

Lila followed him, sinking into the plush cushions. He turned to face her, his expression guarded.

"Evelyn and I were negotiating a merger," he admitted, his voice low. "My gallery has been struggling financially, and I thought joining forces with Evelyn could be a solution.

Lila's eyes widened in surprise. A merger? That was unexpected. She was sure Sam would have told her about a merger. "But why would that lead to such a heated argument?"

"She seemed open to it at first. We had actually gone through all the negotiations and drawn up the contract. All that was left was to sign the final papers. "

Lila leaned forward, her elbows resting on her knees. "But something went wrong."

Graham nodded, his eyes fixated on a distant point. "Evelyn suddenly pulled out of the deal. No explanation, no warning. She left me in a very precarious position."

Lila's brow furrowed as she processed Graham's words. "And that's what you were arguing about at the gallery? Her backing out of the deal?"

Graham nodded, his jaw clenching. "I admit, I lost my temper. I had been relying on this merger."

Lila's mind raced, her voice tinged with suspicion as she pressed on. "Evelyn's decision to back out... that could have been a motive for someone to kill her, couldn't it?"

Graham's head snapped to Lila, his eyes locking with hers. "What are you implying?"

"I'm not implying anything," Lila said evenly. "But you have to admit, the timing is suspicious. Evelyn pulls out of a deal that could have saved your gallery, and then she turns up dead?"

She could see the wheels turning in Graham's mind, the realization dawning on his face. His gallery's future hung in the balance, and Evelyn's death had only brought him more stress.

Graham's eyes flashed with indignation as he stood from the couch. "How dare you accuse me of being involved in Evelyn's murder?" His voice rose, echoing through the gallery. "I would never resort to violence, no matter how desperate my situation might be!"

Lila held her ground, her gaze unwavering. She studied Graham's body language, noting the way his eyes darted around the room, never quite meeting her own. His fingers fidgeted with the cuff of his tailored suit, betraying his unease.

"I'm not accusing you of anything, Graham," Lila said calmly, her voice laced with determination. "But you have to admit, your financial troubles, the failed merger, and the argument with Evelyn at the gallery give you a motive."

Graham scoffed, his lips curling into a scowl. "A motive?"

He paced the length of the gallery, his footsteps punctuating the tense silence. Lila watched him, her eyes tracking his agitated movements.

Her instincts screamed at her, telling her that he was hiding something.

"I may have been in a difficult position," Graham conceded, his voice strained. "But I would never hurt Evelyn. She was a respected colleague, a friend even."

Lila raised an eyebrow, her skepticism evident. "A friend who left you high and dry when you needed her most?"

Graham's jaw clenched, his eyes narrowing. He stopped his pacing, turning to face Lila directly. "You're a new artist. You don't understand the complexities of the art world, the delicate balance of power and influence."

"Then help me understand, Graham," Lila pressed, taking a step closer. "Help me figure out the truth."

Graham's gaze flickered, a momentary crack in his composure. Lila could see the gears turning in his mind, weighing his options. The tension in the room grew, the air thick with unspoken secrets.

But before she could push further, Graham's defenses snapped back into place. He straightened his posture, his expression hardening. "I've told you all I know, Lila. If you want to find Evelyn's killer, you'll have to look somewhere else."

Lila held his gaze for a long moment, the tension between them almost tangible. She knew she couldn't force Graham to reveal more than he was willing, but she also knew that his evasiveness only fueled her suspicion.

With her voice steady and probing. "Where were you on the night of Evelyn's murder, Graham?"

Graham's shoulders stiffened, his gaze darting away for a fleeting moment. "I... I was out of town. Having dinner with a friend."

"Out of town? A friend?" Lila raised an eyebrow, her tone laced with skepticism. "Can anyone confirm your whereabouts?"

Graham's fingers tapped against his thigh, a subtle hint of his frustration with the conversation. "Yes, my friend from Oakwood Valley is going on an extended vacation and will be gone for about six weeks. We were having dinner before he left the country. It might be difficult to reach him now though."

Convenient, Lila thought, her suspicion growing with each passing second.

She studied Graham's body language, noting the way he shifted his weight from one foot to the other, his eyes refusing to meet hers for more than a few seconds at a time. It was a stark contrast to his usual confident demeanor.

"And where exactly did you have this dinner?" Lila pressed, her voice calm but relentless. "Which restaurant?"

Graham hesitated, his brow furrowing as if trying to recall the details. "It was a small hole-in-the-wall place in Oakwood Valley. I don't remember the name off the top of my head. And my friend paid with cash"

Lila's instincts screamed that something wasn't added up. Graham's inability to provide concrete information, his fidgety behavior, it all pointed to a man with something to hide.

"I see," Lila said, her tone measured. "Well, if you do remember the address or any other details about that night, please let me know. It could be crucial to the investigation."

Graham clenched his jaw tight. "Why would I tell you? Why not the police?"

Lila could sense the conversation had reached its limit, that pushing Graham further would only cause him to shut down completely. She needed to regroup, to analyze the information she had gathered and plan her next move.

With a final nod, Lila stood to leave, her mind already whirring with possibilities. Graham's alibi was flimsy at best.

"Thank you for your time, Graham," Lila said, her voice carefully neutral as she turned toward the door. "I appreciate you speaking with me."

Lila's shoes clicked against the polished concrete floor as she made her way towards the gallery's exit, her mind churning with the implications of Graham's flimsy alibi.

She paused, turning to face him one last time. "Graham, I know you and Evelyn had your differences, but I also know how much she respected you and your gallery. I hope, for everyone's sake, that your alibi checks out."

Graham's eyes narrowed, his shoulders stiffening. "Are you implying something, Lila? Because if you are, I'd prefer you just come out and say it."

"I'm not implying anything," Lila replied, her voice cool and even. "I'm just trying to piece together what happened to Evelyn. And right now, your story has a few holes."

"Well, I've told you everything I know, just like I told the police," Graham said, his tone defensive. "I'm sorry I can't be of more help, but as I said, my friend is out of town. It's not like I can just snap my fingers and make him appear."

Lila nodded, her expression thoughtful. "I understand. But you have to admit, it's a bit convenient. Your only alibi is suddenly unavailable."

Lila couldn't help but think it was all too easy. That Graham couldn't remember the name of the restaurant, or that his friend paid in cash, leaving no paper trail. It seemed almost too perfect, as if it had been planned out.

Graham's face flushed, his eyes flashing with anger. "You are grasping at straws, Lila. I had nothing to do with Evelyn's death, and I resent the implication that I did."

Lila held up her hands in a placated gesture. "Graham. I'm just trying to get to the truth. And right now, the truth is proving to be rather elusive."

She turned to leave, her mind already racing ahead to her next steps. She needed to dig deeper into Graham, to see if there were any other inconsistencies in his story.

Lila turned back to face him, her mind already racing with what the next steps in the investigation need to be. "Thank you for your time, Graham," she said, her voice tinged with a mix of suspicion and determination. Her blue eyes lingered on his face for a moment, searching for any hint of deception.

Graham watched Lila, a mix of frustration and uncertainty crossing his face. He raked his fingers through his hair, messing up its careful style. "Lila, wait," he called out, his voice strained.

She paused, turning to face him with a raised eyebrow. "Yes?"

"I... I just want you to know that I had nothing to do with Evelyn's death. We may have had our differences, but I would never hurt her." Graham's words tumbled out in a rush, his usually composed demeanor cracking under the weight of Lila's scrutiny.

Lila studied him for a long moment. She could sense his nerves, but she couldn't understand why. If he had nothing to hide, why was he nervous?

"I'll keep that in mind," she said aloud, her tone carefully neutral. "But I hope you understand that I have to figure out what happened to her, no matter where it takes me."

Graham nodded, his jaw clenching. "Of course. I wouldn't expect anything less from you, Lila. You always were tenacious."

A ghost of a smile flickered across Lila's face.

She turned to leave once more, her skirt swishing around her ankles as she walked out into the bright sunlight. She squinted against the bright sun. Her mind raced as she replayed the conversation, analyzing every word, every gesture. Graham's alibi was shaky at best, and his nervousness only fueled her suspicions. But she couldn't shake the feeling.

The streets of Willow Creek seemed to pulse with a newfound energy as Lila strode away from Graham's gallery, her mind full of revelations and suspicions.

Graham's alibi, his financial problems, Evelyn's sudden decision to pull out of the merger... none of it made sense. Nothing added up.

CHAPTER 8

Lila stepped into Adrian's studio the next morning, the air heavy with the scent of fresh paint. Canvases leaned against the walls in various stages of completion. Maxine followed closely behind, her sharp gaze taking in every detail.

Adrian stood before a large abstract painting, his brush hovering hesitantly over the canvas. He glanced up as they approached, his eyes darting away just as quickly. "Lila, I wasn't expecting you."

"We thought we'd drop by and see how you are holding up after the gallery show was postponed," Lila said, her tone light. "Have you met Maxine? She's an old friend of Evelyn's."

Adrian's eyes flicked nervously between Lila and Maxine. "Nice to meet you," he mumbled, before turning back to his canvas.

She stepped closer to the painting, studying the chaotic blend of colors and shapes. "This piece is amazing. Is it part of your new collection?"

Adrian nodded curtly, his brush still poised in midair. "Yeah, it's one of the centerpieces." He turned away, busying himself with rearranging his paintbrushes, his movements sharp and agitated.

Lila frowned, puzzled by his curt response. Adrian had always been passionate talking about his work. This aloof attitude was a stark contrast to the banter they usually shared.

She exchanged a glance with Maxine, who raised an eyebrow, clearly sensing the same unease. Lila cleared her throat, determined to press on. "I can't wait to see how it all comes together."

Adrian shrugged, his gaze fixed on the paint-splattered floor. "Thanks. I'm just trying to do my part." His fingers fidgeted with a tube of paint, squeezing it with unnecessary force.

Lila watched him closely, his hunched shoulders, a tapping foot, the way he seemed to be ready to snap. Something was definitely off.

She took a step closer, her voice softening. "Adrian, is everything alright? You seem a bit...on edge."

He flinched at her words, his eyes finally meeting hers for a fleeting moment. In that brief instant, Lila caught a glimpse worry beneath the surface. But just as quickly, he looked away, his jaw clenching.

"I'm fine. Just stressed about the show, that's all." Adrian turned back to his painting, his brush slashing across the canvas with a sudden savagery. "Look, I appreciate you checking in, but I really need to focus on getting this finished."

Lila hesitated, torn between pushing further and respecting his obvious desire to be left alone. She glanced at Maxine, who gave a subtle shake of her head, signaling that maybe now was not the time to press the issue.

With a sigh, Lila nodded. "Of course. We'll let you get back to work. Just remember, if there's anything you need, anything at all, we're here for you."

Adrian grunted in response, his attention fully absorbed by the painting before him.

Lila and Maxine turned to leave, but as they neared the door, Lila paused, her hand resting on the handle. The nagging feeling in her gut refused to subside.

She glanced back at Adrian, who stood motionless before his canvas, his brush lifted in hesitation. The silence stretched between them, heavy with unspoken secrets and unanswered questions. Lila glanced at Maxine, whose piercing gaze was fixed on Adrian's back.

In that moment, a silent understanding passed between the two women. They couldn't leave, not yet.

Lila turned back, her footsteps soft against the paint-splattered floor as she approached Adrian once more. He tensed visibly at the sound of her approach, his grip tightening on the paintbrush until his knuckles turned white.

"Adrian," she said softly, "we know something's bothering you. And it's not just the show, is it?"

Adrian's shoulders sagged, the fight draining out of him as he turned around. He set the paintbrush down with a heavy sigh, his eyes fixed on the canvas. "No, it's not just the show," he admitted.

Lila fixed Adrian with a piercing stare, her blue eyes unwavering. "Is there anything you know that could explain Julian's remarks, the one about Evelyn making 'interesting enemies'?"

Adrian's hands, already fidgeting with a paintbrush, stilled. "I don't know what you're talking about." His voice was tight, defensive.

"Come on, Adrian," Lila pressed, taking a step closer. "He's a gossip, but Julian doesn't make comments like that without a reason. What happened between you and Evelyn?"

Adrian's gaze darted around the studio, landing anywhere but on Lila's face. The silence stretched, thick with tension. Lila could almost hear the gears turning in his head, weighing his options.

Finally, he sighed in defeat. "I owed her money; more specifically I owe the gallery," he admitted, his voice barely above a whisper. "A lot of money."

Lila's eyebrows shot up, surprise mingling with a growing sense of unease. "What for?"

Adrian ran a hand through his hair, leaving a streak of blue paint in its wake. "She'd been helping me out, you know? Covering some of my expenses so I could focus on my art." He gestured around the studio at the half-finished canvases and scattered supplies. "But it was starting to add up, and I couldn't pay her back as fast as we originally agreed on."

Lila exchanged a glance with Maxine, who had been quietly observing the exchange.

"So, you had a disagreement about how the loan would be repaid?" Lila asked, her tone carefully neutral.

Adrian nodded, his gaze fixed on the floor. "She was getting impatient. She said I was behind on my payments, and that there was something that she needed the money for. I tried to explain that I was doing my best, but…" He trailed off, shaking his head.

Lila's mind raced, trying to place this new information with what they already knew. Evelyn had always been generous with her artists, but she was also a shrewd businesswoman. If Adrian had fallen behind on his payments, it could have strained their relationship.

"Look, I know how it sounds, but we finally had it all worked out. I was going to pay her back in full with the money from the show." He gestured towards the paintings around him, a hint of desperation creeping into his voice. "She knew that. She agreed to it."

Lila nodded slowly, processing this new information. While it was clear that Adrian and Evelyn's relationship had been strained by the debt, his insistence that they had reached an agreement was compelling. Still, something about his demeanor left her unsettled.

She glanced at Maxine, silently communicating her thoughts. They would need to dig deeper, to find out just how serious this disagreement had been, and whether it could have escalated into something more sinister.

Lila's intuition nagged at her, urging her to probe further. She leaned forward, her eyes locked on Adrian's. "I understand that you had an agreement, but sometimes these situations can escalate beyond money. Did you feel like the debt had become something more personal between you and Evelyn?"

Adrian's eyes widened, and for a moment, Lila thought she saw a flicker of panic. But he quickly composed himself, shaking his head vehemently. "No, no. It was never like that. Sure, we had our disagreements, but Evelyn was always professional. She wouldn't have let a loan turn into a personal vendetta."

Lila raised an eyebrow, unconvinced. "But what about from your side? Did you ever feel like the pressure of the loan was becoming too much? That maybe, in a moment of desperation, you might have considered something drastic?"

"What? No!" Adrian's voice rose, echoing in the quiet studio. "Look, I know I was in a tough spot, but I would never have hurt Evelyn. My loan was technically with the gallery. The show was going to generate enough money to pay her back and then some. If something were to happen to Evelyn, I would still owe the money to the new owner. She was my ticket out of this mess. Why would I jeopardize that?"

He began to pace, his hands gesturing wildly as he spoke. "Besides, even if I wanted to do something stupid, which I didn't, I couldn't afford to risk it. If anything happened to Evelyn, the show would have been cancelled, and then where would I be? The next owner may not be as understanding."

Lila watched him carefully, noting the way his body seemed to vibrate with nervous energy. She glanced at Maxine, who was studying Adrian with equal intensity. They both knew that desperation could drive people to do unthinkable things, but Adrian's logic was sound. Hurting Evelyn would have only made his situation worse.

She decided to change tactics, to give Adrian a chance to collect himself. "I apologize if I came across as accusatory, Adrian. We're just trying to understand the full picture here. I know how much this show means to you, and I can only imagine the stress you must be under."

Adrian stopped pacing, his shoulders slumping as he turned to face her. "I'm sorry too. I didn't mean to snap. It's just... this whole situation, it's a lot to handle. I cared about Evelyn, and I would never have wanted anything bad to happen to her."

Lila fixed Adrian with a steady gaze. "Where were you the night Evelyn was killed?"

Adrian's eyes widened, "I... I was here. In my studio. Working."

"Can anyone confirm that?" Maxine asked.

He shook his head, a bead of sweat forming on his brow despite the cool air in the gallery. "No. I was alone. I often work late into the night when I'm prepping for a show."

Lila watched him closely, noting the way his fingers twitched, the slight tremble in his voice. "Oh, Adrian. You have to understand how this looks."

"I had nothing to do with Evelyn's death!" Adrian's voice rose, echoing off the walls. "Yes, we had our differences, but I would never hurt her. She was my ticket out of this financial mess. Hurting her would've been stupid."

"We're not accusing you of anything, Adrian," Lila said gently. "We're just trying to understand your relationship with Evelyn and if there was anyone who might have wanted to harm her."

Adrian took a deep breath, his shoulders slumping in defeat. "I honestly can't think of anyone who would want to hurt her. She was well-liked in the art community and she didn't have any enemies that I know of."

Lila studied Adrian's face, noting the genuine distress in his eyes. While his lack of an alibi was concerning, his logic about hurting Evelyn being against his own interests made sense.

"We want to believe you, Adrian," Lila said softly, trying to ease the tension. "But you have to understand our position. We're just trying to figure out what happened."

Adrian ran a hand through his hair again, leaving another streak of blue paint in its wake. "I know. I know. But I swear to you, I had nothing to do with this. I may be desperate, but I'm not a killer."

"We appreciate your honesty, Adrian," Lila said, her tone measured. "If you think of anything else, anything at all that might be relevant, please let me know."

Adrian nodded, his shoulders slumping as if a weight had been lifted. "I will. I promise."

As Lila and Maxine turned to leave, Lila couldn't help but glance back over her shoulder. Adrian had already returned to his work, his brush moving furiously across the canvas.

Lila and Maxine walked in silence through the studio. As they reached the exit, Maxine finally spoke. "He's hiding something."

Lila's brow furrowed in thought. "I'm not sure. What else could there be? And why?"

Maxine shrugged, her gaze distant. "Money makes people do desperate things. If he was in deep with Evelyn, who knows what he might have done to get out of it."

Lila sighed, pushing open the door and stepping out into the bright sunlight. "But he was going to pay her back with the show, And the Adrian I know isn't capable of murder?"

"I'm sorry Lila," Maxine said. "But we can't rule it out. The way he was acting, the nervousness, the evasiveness... it's not the behavior of an innocent man."

"True, but it's not a smoking gun either." Lila paused, her hand on Maxine's arm. "We need to be careful about jumping to conclusions. Adrian may be acting suspiciously, but that doesn't necessarily mean he's guilty."

Maxine nodded slowly, her eyes narrowing in thought. "You're right."

Lila sighed, "So, what's our next move?"

"We talk to Julian," Maxine said, her tone decisive. "He's the one who started this whole 'interesting enemies' thing. Maybe he knows something we don't."

Lila's stomach twisted at the thought of facing the art critic again. But she knew they had no choice. "Okay, let's do it." Lila said, "But, before we talk to Julian we should update Detective Reed on what we have found so far."

Maxine raised an eyebrow. "Are you sure that's wise? We don't want to tip off the police to our investigation. They might try to stop us."

Lila shook her head firmly. "No, we need to keep Detective Reed in the loop. We're not police, Maxine. If we stumble onto something important, they need to know."

Maxine pursed her lips, clearly not entirely convinced. "Alright, I guess you have a point, but let's give it a day to talk to the detective. Then we can track down Julian after that."

CHAPTER 9

L ila's fingers hovered over her phone, the bright screen illuminating her determined expression in the dim afternoon light of her studio. She typed out a message to Detective Reed, her words infused with the unwavering confidence that had driven her investigation thus far.

"I have some new information about Evelyn's case. Can we meet at the coffee shop in an hour?"

Her thumb paused for a moment before hitting send. Lila knew she had told Maxine that she would give it a day, but she couldn't wait. The response came quickly, as if he had been waiting.

"I'll be there."

Lila slipped the phone into her pocket, a mixture of anticipation and nervousness coiling in her stomach.

Lila's footsteps echoed through the quiet streets of Willow Creek, her mind racing with conflicting thoughts. On one hand, she couldn't shake the evidence she had gathered - Graham's financial troubles and the fact that Evelyn backed out of the merger, Adrian's mounting debts to Evelyn's gallery. But on the other hand, these were the same men she had worked with for years.

The late afternoon sun cast long shadows across the sidewalk as Lila approached the coffee shop. She spotted Detective Reed through the widow sitting at a table in the corner, his broad shoulders hunched forward, elbows resting on the table. He looked up as she walked through the door, a small bell announcing her arrival. His blue eyes watched her approach, sharp and assessing.

"Detective Reed," Lila greeted him with a nod. She sat down beside him, leaving a respectable distance between them.

"Call me Marcus. What have you got, Lila?" Marcus asked, his tone measured.

Lila met his gaze, her own eyes flashing with determination. "I've been asking around, seeing if I could find out anything new."

She launched into her findings, outlining Graham's financial struggles and Adrian's debt, giving both men a motive to kill Evelyn. As she spoke, Lila felt a growing sense of satisfaction. She was onto something. Marcus would have to take her seriously.

But as she finished, Lila noticed the look on Marcus's face. It wasn't the impressed or grateful expression she had been hoping for. Instead, he looked … tired, resigned, even.

"Lila," he began, his voice low and serious. Marcus leaned back, folding his arms across his chest. "We already know about Graham's financial situation and Adrian's debt. But there's more to an investigation than just potential motives."

Lila's brows furrowed, a flicker of frustration igniting within her. "But, either one of them could have killed her. It's a solid lead."

"It's a theory," Marcus countered, his tone firm. "And one that requires evidence to back it up. Lila, I appreciate your dedication, but you need to let us handle this."

Lila opened her mouth to protest, but Marcus held up a hand, silencing her. "I know you want to help, but you're not a trained detective. There are procedures, protocols, and potentially dangerous situations that can come up in a murder investigation that you aren't trained to handle."

A wave of indignation surged through Lila. She had worked hard to uncover this information, and now Marcus was dismissing her like some meddling kid. She straightened her spine, meeting his gaze head-on.

"I may not be a detective, but I know these people. And right now, my instincts are telling me that Graham and Adrian are key to solving this case. You can't just ignore that."

Marcus sighed, rubbing a hand over his face. "I'm not ignoring anything. But I need you to trust me, Lila. Trust that we're doing our jobs and that we'll follow every lead, including the ones you've brought to me."

Lila bit her lip, torn between her desire to push further and the realization that Marcus was not going to budge. She knew he was just looking out for her, but it didn't make it any easier to step back.

"Fine," she said at last, her tone clipped. "But if you find out anything else, you'll let me know?"

Marcus hesitated, then nodded. "I will. But in return, you need to promise me you'll stay out of this from now on. No more investigating, no more questioning people."

Lila didn't respond, her mind already whirling with the next steps she wanted to take. She couldn't just sit back and do nothing, not when she knew there was more to the story.

Marcus seemed to sense her reluctance. He leaned forward, his expression grave. "I mean it, Lila. If you keep pushing, you could end up in serious trouble. Or worse, you could become the killer's next target."

Lila nodded slowly, her blue eyes meeting Marcus's concerned gaze. "I understand, Marcus."

Marcus's brow furrowed, his blue eyes piercing as he fixed Lila with a stern gaze. "I need you to listen to me, Lila. Really listen." His voice was low, urgent. "This isn't some puzzle for you to solve. These are people we're dealing with. Dangerous people."

Lila met his gaze unflinchingly, her own eyes alight with determination. "I know that, Marcus. But I can't just sit back and do nothing. Not when I might be able to help."

"Help?" Marcus shook his head, frustration evident in the set of his jaw. "You could be putting yourself in serious danger. If you keep poking around, asking questions, you might end up tipping off the killer. And then what? You think they'll just let you walk away?"

Lila's heart raced at the thought, but she refused to back down. "I'm being careful. I know how to handle myself."

"Do you?" Marcus leaned closer. "Because from where I'm sitting, it looks like you're in over your head. You're not a detective, Lila."

Lila could see the genuine concern in his eyes. For a moment, doubt crept in, whispering that maybe he was right. Maybe she should step back, let the professionals handle it.

But then she thought of Evelyn, of the unanswered questions surrounding her death. She thought of the connections she had already made, the pieces of the puzzle that were slowly falling into place.

"I can't just walk away," she said softly, her voice filled with quiet conviction. "I know I might be risking a lot. But if there's even a chance that I could help bring Evelyn's killer to justice... I have to try."

Marcus sighed heavily, rubbing a hand over his face. "I can't stop you. I know that. But I'm begging you, Lila. Be careful. Don't take any unnecessary risks. And if you find anything, anything at all... come to me first. Don't try to handle it on your own."

Lila nodded, a flicker of warmth spreading through her at his words.

"I will," she promised. "I'll be careful. And I'll come to you with anything I find."

A chill ran down Lila's spine at his words, but she brushed it aside. She was too far into this to back out now. One way or another, she would see this investigation through to the end.

Lila stood, the legs of her chair scraping against the tiled floor. She couldn't sit here any longer, listening to Marcus's warnings and feeling the weight of his disapproval. She needed to move, to think, to plan her next steps.

"I have to go," Lila said, her voice tight.

She turned on her heel and strode out of the coffee shop, the bell above the door jingling in her wake. Lila's fingers tightened around the strap of her bag as she walked away from Marcus, her mind reeling with the implications of their conversation. She could feel his gaze boring into her back, a silent warning to heed his advice. But even as guilt niggled at her conscience, determination surged through her veins.

She couldn't just sit back and watch from the sidelines, not when Evelyn's killer was still out there. Lila's steps quickened as she made her way down the street, the bustling sounds of the town's main street fading into the background as her thoughts raced ahead.

Marcus's words echoed in her mind, a reminder of the dangers that lurked beneath the surface of this case. She was sure there was something the police were missing

With a deep breath, Lila continued down the street, her mind already whirring with the next steps in her investigation.

As she walked, she pictured Graham and Adrian, both with their own potential motives, both with secrets they were desperate to keep hidden.

She would have to be more careful. She would verify her information, double-check her sources, and tread lightly when confronting those who might have something to hide. And if she found anything truly urgent or dangerous, she would go straight to Marcus, just as he had asked.

CHAPTER 10

Lila stabbed at her salad, a frown etched across her brow. "I just don't understand where Julian could be." She glanced up at Samantha, her blue eyes narrowed in frustration. "No one seems to have seen him since the night Evelyn was murdered, and he's not answering when I try to call him."

Samantha leaned in close, her voice soothed. "I know it's been frustrating, but we'll find him. Julian will turn up and we can ask him what he may know about Evelyn's death then."

Lila sighed heavily and set down her fork. It had been two days since she had met with Marcus to tell him what they knew so far, and neither she nor Maxine had been able to find Julian. She tucked a stray lock of blond hair behind her ear, a habit that emerged whenever her mind was churning. "I feel like we're hitting a wall, Sam. Graham and Adrian both have motives, but nothing concrete to tie them to the murder."

"Then let's go over what we know so far. Maybe that will help." Samantha leaned forward, her voice low. "Graham was struggling financially. He stood to gain a lot from merging with Evelyn's gallery, which he lost when she backed out."

"You really had no idea about a merger?" Lila asked.

"Not a clue." Sam replied frustrated. "As her assistant, I should have known these types of things. Maybe she had always planned to back out, and that's why I didn't know about it."

"Maybe," Lila nodded, her thoughts drifting to the nervous artist. "And then there's Adrian. He was in debt to Evelyn, constantly on edge. But would that be enough for him to kill her?"

"Neither of them seems fully trustworthy," Samantha mused, taking a sip of her iced tea. "But we can't rule them out just yet."

Lila's gaze drifted to the bustling diner around them, watching as patrons chatted and laughed

"I just wish I could talk to Julian," Lila said, her voice tinged with exasperation. "He was being so cryptic that day, hinting at something."

Samantha offered a sympathetic smile. "Maybe he's afraid of getting involved. Or perhaps he doesn't realize that he knows something."

"We can't lose hope," Samantha said, as if sensing Lila's mounting frustration. "The truth will come out eventually. We just need to keep digging."

Lila nodded.

Samantha's eyes suddenly widened, her gaze fixed on a point just over Lila's shoulder. "Speak of the devil," she whispered, a hint of excitement in her voice. "Julian just walked in."

Lila's heart skipped a beat. She slowly turned, following Samantha's gaze to the diner's entrance. There he was, Julian Thompson, looking as impeccable as ever in a tailored suit, his dark hair perfectly styled. He strode towards the take-out counter, seemingly oblivious to the two women watching him intently.

"This might be our chance," Samantha said, leaning forward. "We could ask him to join us while he waits for his food."

Lila hesitated, her mind racing. She knew Julian's reputation for being a gossip, but Samantha was right. This could be their only opportunity to catch him off guard and get some answers. She glanced back at Julian, who was now placing his order with the waitress.

"Okay," Lila said, determination settling in her voice. "Let's do it."

Lila took a deep breath and stood up, smoothing her skirt. She approached Julian at the counter, "Julian," Lila said, her voice steady despite the nerves fluttering in her stomach. "It's good to see you."

Julian turned, his eyebrows raised in mild surprise. "Lila," he acknowledged with a nod. "I didn't expect to see you here."

"We were just having lunch," Lila explained, gesturing towards their table where Sam was still seated. "Would you like to join us while you wait?"

Julian hesitated for a moment, his gaze flickering between Lila and the take-out counter. "I suppose I have a few minutes," he said finally, his tone carefully neutral.

Lila led him back to the table, where Samantha greeted him with a warm smile.

Julian slid into the booth beside Samantha, his piercing gaze settling on Lila.

"So, to what do I owe this impromptu lunch invitation?" Julian asked, his tone laced with a hint of skepticism.

Lila exchanged a quick glance with Samantha before speaking. "We wanted to ask you about something you said the day before Evelyn died. About Evelyn having 'interesting enemies'."

Julian leaned back, a flicker of understanding crossing his features. "Ah. I remember that conversation."

"We were hoping you could elaborate on what you meant," Samantha chimed in, her voice gentle but probing.

Julian reclined in his chair, a sly smile appearing on his face. "Really? The art world is not for the weak. It's a ruthless industry, fueled by hidden agendas and deceit."

Lila leaned forward, her elbows resting on the table. "I'm beginning to see that," she said, her voice lowering conspiratorially, "I overheard some interesting rumors. Something about Adrian and his... financial troubles?"

Julian's eyes narrowed, a flicker of annoyance crossing his features. "Ah, Adrian. A tortured artist with a knack for drama." He shrugged, his shoulders rising and falling with a practiced nonchalance. "It's no secret that he's had his fair share of struggles. But then again, who hasn't in this business?"

Samantha cleared her throat, her quiet voice cutting through the tension. "We were just wondering if you knew anything else," she said, her tone gentle yet probing. "It sounded like there might be more to the story."

Julian sighed, his fingers drumming against the tabletop. "Look, I don't make it a habit to gossip about my colleagues," he said, his words measured and careful. "But if you must know, Adrian has always been a bit... unpredictable. He's had his ups and downs with Evelyn over the years, mostly related to money."

"So, you're saying Adrian had a motive?" Lila asked, focusing on keeping her voice steady, not believing for a second that Julian didn't like to gossip.

Julian held up a hand, his expression turning serious. "Let's not jump to conclusions," he said. "Adrian may be many things, but a murderer? I highly doubt it. The man can barely keep his own life together."

Lila sat back, her brow furrowed in thought. Julian's words made sense. The more she talked to Julian the more resolved she became that Adrian didn't do this, despite what Maxine thinks.

Lila's gaze drifted back to Julian, her mind shifting gears. "What about Graham Whitaker?" she asked, her voice steady despite the flutter of nerves in her stomach. "I know he and Evelyn had their differences, but could there be more to it than just a professional rivalry?"

Julian's eyes narrowed, a flicker of something unreadable crossing his features. He leaned in, his voice dropping to a conspiratorial whisper. "Actually, now that you mention it, I did hear a rather interesting rumor while I was in New York for an art show the night Evelyn was murdered."

Lila's heart skipped a beat, her fingers tightening around her coffee mug. "Go on," she urged, trying to keep the eagerness out of her voice.

"Well, according to my sources, Graham had initially tried to completely take over Evelyn's gallery, long before his financial troubles became public knowledge," Julian revealed, his words heavy with implication. "Apparently, settling on the idea of just a merger was a bitter pill for him to swallow, especially since he originally had his sights set on owning Evelyn's gallery outright."

Lila's mind reeled with this new information, the pieces of the puzzle slowly clicking into place - the reason for Graham's resentment.

She leaned forward, her elbows resting on the table as she fixed Julian with an intense stare. "So, you're saying that Graham had a motive for wanting Evelyn out of the picture?" she asked, her voice barely above a whisper.

Julian shrugged, his expression unreadable. "I'm not saying anything definitive," he said, his words carefully chosen. "But it does raise some interesting questions about Graham's true intentions, doesn't it?"

Lila sat back, her mind racing with the implications of Julian's words. She glanced at Samantha, who seemed equally stunned by the revelation. They needed to dig deeper, to uncover the truth behind Graham's actions and his possible involvement in Evelyn's murder.

But even as the possibility of a new lead coursed through her mind, Lila couldn't shake the nagging feeling that there was still more to this than meets the eye.

As they sat in silence, each lost in their own thoughts, Julian's gaze drifted to the counter where his food was being prepared. He drummed his fingers on the table, a pensive look on his face.

"You know," he began, his voice low and conspiratorial, "I don't think Graham or Adrian had anything to do with Evelyn's murder."

Lila's head turned back to Julian, her eyes narrowing as she studied Julian's expression. "What do you mean?" she asked.

Julian leaned back, crossing his arms over his chest. "Think about it," he said, his tone almost patronizing. "Evelyn had a long career in the art world. She made enemies, burned bridges, and stepped on more than a few toes along the way."

Lila's mind raced as she considered Julian's words. It was true that Evelyn had a reputation for being tough, uncompromising, and sometimes even ruthless in her pursuit of success.

"So, you think the killer is someone from Evelyn's past?" Lila asked.

Julian nodded, a knowing smirk playing at the corners of his mouth. "It's just a theory," he said, "but I wouldn't be surprised if it was an artist she disagreed with or someone holding a long-standing grudge."

Lila's mind whirled with the possibilities. Julian's revelation opened up a new realm of possibility. If he was right, then they had been chasing the wrong person.

She opened her mouth to press him further, but before she could speak, the waitress called out Julian's name from behind the counter. His food was ready.

Julian stood, smoothing the creases in his impeccable suit. "Well, that's my cue," he said, his voice dripping with his usual sarcasm. "It's been a pleasure, ladies."

Lila watched as he sauntered over to the counter, her mind still reeling from his revelations. She turned to Samantha, her eyes wide with a mix of excitement and trepidation.

"What do you think?" she asked.

Samantha shook her head, her expression thoughtful. "I don't know," she admitted. "But what Julian said about Graham trying to take over Evelyn's gallery completely... that's news to me."

"I think we need to start digging into Evelyn's past. If Julian is right, then we've been looking in the wrong direction all along."

Lila watched as Julian exited the diner, the bell above the door jingling in his wake. She turned back to Samantha, her brow furrowed in thought.

"I don't know what to make of all this," Lila admitted, her fingers absently tracing the rim of her coffee mug. "Julian's theory about an artist from Evelyn's past... it's possible, but where do we even start looking with that? And I'm not sure I'm ready to give up on Graham just yet"

Samantha leaned back in the booth, her eyes distant. "Evelyn had had a long career, and she had worked with countless artists over the years. It could be anyone."

Lila sighed, feeling the weight of the investigation pressing down on her. "Maybe we should start with the gallery records," she suggested, her mind already racing with possibilities. "If we can find a list of all the artists Evelyn worked with, we might be able to narrow it down to those who had a falling out with her, or maybe someone she rejected."

Samantha nodded, her expression thoughtful. "It's a place to start, at least. The police finally said I can get back inside. I can head to the gallery and start digging through the files. You should keep looking into Graham, just in case. We can't rule him out completely, but I don't think Adrian had anything to do with it."

"Me neither," Lila agreed. Julian's words echoed in her mind.

As they slid out of the booth and made their way to the door, Lila couldn't shake the feeling that they were moving in the right direction finally.

She stepped out into the bright sunlight, squinting against the glare. The street was bustling with activity, but Lila felt disconnected from it all, her mind lost in theories and suspicions.

"We'll figure this out," Samantha said, placing a comforted hand on Lila's arm.

Lila nodded, turning to face Samantha, her blue eyes shining with apprehension. "Are you sure you're okay to go to the gallery alone?" she asked, her voice tinged with concern.

Samantha gave Lila a reassuring smile. "I'll be fine," she said. "The police have already been through the gallery. I'm just nervous."

Lila nodded, understanding the determination in her friend's eyes. "Okay," she relented. "But call me if you need anything, alright?"

With a final hug, the two women parted ways. Lila watched as Samantha strode off down the sidewalk, her chestnut ponytail swinging with each purposeful step.

Lila's mind raced as she walked back through town to her studio, the information from Julian running through her mind. She needed to talk to Graham again, to dig deeper into his history with Evelyn and uncover any secrets he might be hiding.

As Lila approached her studio door, her mind still swirling with the revelations from Julian, she stopped short. Her heart skipped a beat as her eyes locked onto a photograph taped to the weathered wood of her door. The image was crisp and clear, capturing a moment from just a hour ago - Lila, Samantha, and Julian huddled together in deep conversation in the diner.

Lila's fingers trembled as she reached out to touch it, her breath catching in her throat. Her heart pounded in her chest as she stared at the photograph, a chill running down her spine. Someone had been watching her, or them, following their every move. And now they wanted her to know it.

With shaking hands, she carefully peeled the photo from the door, her eyes scanning the area for any sign of the person who left it. The street was quiet, with only a few passersby going about their day, oblivious to Lila's growing panic.

She quickly unlocked her studio door and slipped inside, locking it behind her. Leaning against the door, she took several deep breaths, trying to calm her racing heart. Her eyes darted around the familiar space of her studio, searching for anything out of place, any sign that someone had been there.

Everything seemed to be in its place - canvases leaning against the walls, paintbrushes scattered across her work table, the familiar scent of oil paints hanging in the air. Her breathing slowed.

Lila's mind raced as she tried to make sense of the photograph. Who could have taken it? And more importantly, why? Was she getting close? Her fingers tightened around the glossy paper, crinkling it slightly.

The only person she thought had any real reason to kill Evelyn was Graham.

Her trembling hand reached for her phone, fingers frantically scrolling through her contacts until she found Graham's number. Her heart raced as she hovered over the call button, feeling a surge of fear and apprehension pulsing through her body. She took a deep breath and pressed the button, adrenaline coursing through her veins as she waited for Graham to pick up. It rang three times before Graham's voice filled the line.

"Lila," Graham paused. "What a surprise. I wasn't expecting to hear from you so soon."

"Graham, I need to talk to you. It's important." Lila's tone was firm, hiding her fear and leaving no room for argument.

There was a pause, a moment of hesitation. "Of course. Why don't you come by my gallery this afternoon? We can discuss whatever's on your mind."

Lila agreed, ending the call with a sense of determination. She would get to the bottom of this.

As she moved deeper into her studio, Lila's phone buzzed with an incoming text. It was from Samantha.

"Hey, I'm at the gallery, everything looks ok here. I also decided that I'm going to rescheduling the show in Evelyn's honor. Wish you were here to help, but I know you will go crazy if you don't talk to Graham. Keep me posted."

Lila's heart ached at the thought of Samantha at the gallery alone. As emotion tightened in her chest, she wished she could be there to help, to honor Evelyn's memory in the way she deserved. But the investigation had to come first.

"Thanks, Sam. I'll keep you updated. Let me know if you need anything," Lila typed back, hitting send with a sigh.

Chapter 11

As Lila stepped into Graham's gallery, sunlight poured through the expansive windows, illuminating the large abstract canvases lining the white walls. Despite the serene atmosphere, tension coiled in Lila's gut. She scanned the room for Graham, bracing herself for the impending conversation.

"Lila, darling!" Graham emerged from behind a partition, arms outstretched in greeting. "So glad you could make it."

Lila forced a smile. "Hello, Graham. Thank you for seeing me, especially after last time." Her trepidation mixed with determination as she studied Graham's face, searching for any sign of guilt or deception.

He waved a dismissive hand. "Of course, of course. Come over here, let me show you the latest pieces from an artist a few towns over."

As Graham launched into an animated description of the painting and its artist as he move farther into the gallery, Lila nodded, absently following him. Her gaze wandered the pristine gallery walls, searching for any signs that might confirm her suspicions about Graham's involvement in Evelyn's death or sending her that photo.

Lila shook her head slightly, refocusing on the task at hand. She couldn't let her suspicions overwhelm her, not yet. First, she needed answers about Evelyn's death and the failed merger. She took a deep breath, preparing herself for the inevitable conversation.

"Graham," she interrupted gently, "as much as I'd love to talk about new artists in the area, I'm afraid there's something important we need to talk about..."

Graham's smile faltered for a moment, but he quickly recovered. "Of course, of course. Let's sit and talk." He gestured towards a sleek leather couch at the back of the gallery. "Can I offer you some coffee?"

Lila nodded, settling onto the couch as Graham busied himself with the espresso machine. The normalcy of the act felt surreal, given the circumstances. She watched him work, trying to reconcile this amiable host with the cutthroat businessman she knew him to be and the guarded man she met the last time she was here.

Graham returned, pressing a steaming cup into her hands. "Now, what's on your mind?" He sat across from her, crossing his legs with an air of nonchalance.

Lila took a sip, buying herself a moment to gather her thoughts. "I wanted to check in, see how you and the gallery are holding up."

Graham's expression remained impassive. "It's been difficult, of course. But we must carry on."

Lila noted the detachment in his voice, the way he spoke of Evelyn as if she were a friend, and not a woman he'd fought tooth and nail to outmaneuver. The contradiction unsettled her.

"I can only imagine," she said carefully. "Especially with the merger falling through so suddenly. It must have been quite a blow."

Graham's jaw tightened almost imperceptibly. "A setback, certainly. But in this business, one learns to adapt." He took a measured sip of his coffee. "The gallery will survive, merger or no merger."

Lila studied him over the rim of her cup, searching for cracks in his composure. "I'm sure it will. You've always been resilient, Graham. Determined."

"Determination is key in this industry," he said smoothly. "As I'm sure you know, Lila. Your own career is a testament to that."

Lila inclined her head, acknowledging the deflection.

Lila leaned forward, her tone casual but deliberate. "You know, Graham, I've been hearing some interesting rumors lately. About your business practices, specifically."

Graham's hand paused midway to his mouth, his coffee cup hovering in the air. "Oh? Really?"

"Well, for starters, I heard that you tried to take over Evelyn's gallery. Before the merger was even on the table."

The words hung in the air, sharp and accusatory. Graham lowered his cup slowly, his eyes narrowing. "I'm not sure what you're implying, Lila."

"I'm not implying anything," Lila said, holding his gaze steadily. "I'm just curious. It must have been frustrating, having your plans fall through like that. Especially for someone as ambitious as you."

Graham's jaw tightened, a muscle twitching beneath his skin. "Ambition is hardly a crime."

"No, of course not. But it can lead people to do desperate things, can't it? When they feel like they've been backed into a corner?"

Lila watched as Graham's mask slipped, just for a moment. Beneath the veneer of calm, she caught a glimpse of something raw and angry, a simmering resentment that made her skin prickle.

But just as quickly, it was gone, replaced by a smooth, practiced smile. "Lila, I'm not sure what you've heard, but I can assure you, my intentions with Evelyn's gallery were always aboveboard. The merger was a mutual decision, one that would have benefited us both."

Lila leaned back in her seat, studying him closely. She didn't believe him, not for a second. If the merger was mutual, why did Evelyn back out?

"Of course," she said, her tone light. "I didn't mean to imply otherwise. I'm just trying to understand the situation, that's all."

Graham's smile didn't reach his eyes. "I appreciate your concern, Lila. But I can assure you, there's nothing to understand. Evelyn's death was a tragedy, but it had nothing to do with me or my gallery."

Lila nodded, but inside, her mind was racing. Graham's defensiveness, his carefully chosen words. Even as every instinct screamed that he was lying.

"Of course," she said, her tone conciliatory. "I apologize if I've offended you. It's just that Evelyn was a dear friend, and her death has left so many unanswered questions."

Graham's jaw tightened, a flicker of something dark passing through his eyes. "I'm not sure what you're implying, Lila. But I can assure you, my only concern has always been the success of both our galleries."

Lila held his gaze, refusing to look away. "Of course. I didn't mean to offend. It's just... for someone as competitive as you, it must have been quite a blow. To come so close to getting what you wanted, only to have it slip away at the last moment."

Graham's eyes darkened, his gaze drifting away from Lila's probing stare. "The takeover attempt was just business, Lila. Nothing personal against Evelyn." His voice grew sharper, a hint of anger seeping through his carefully controlled façade. "And again, the merger negotiations were mutual. Beneficial for both parties."

Lila noticed the way his jaw clenched, the slight twitch of his eye. His body language screamed the opposite of his words. She pressed on, sensing a crack in his armor. "But it must have been frustrating, Graham. To have the merger fall through like that, after all your efforts."

He stood abruptly, pacing towards the window. "That's the same question, Lila. The answer is not any different. I don't see how any of this is relevant. Yes, I was disappointed with how things turned out. But I had nothing to gain from Evelyn's death." He turned back to face her, his expression hard. "That gallery show was going to bring new business to both our galleries. Bring in new art collectors to Willow Creek as a whole. They would have come to visit my gallery also. Why would I jeopardize that?"

Lila watched him closely, noting the tension in his shoulders, the way his fingers drummed against his thigh.

"I understand, Graham. I'm just trying to piece together what happened." She softened her tone, trying a different approach. "This must be a difficult time for you, with the future of your gallery so uncertain."

Graham's eyes flashed with something unreadable. "I appreciate your concern, Lila. But I assure you, my gallery will be just fine." He moved towards the door, a clear signal for her to leave. "Now, if you'll excuse me, I have work to attend to."

Lila stood, smoothing her skirt as she followed him to the door. "Of course. Thank you for your time, Graham." She paused at the door, meeting his gaze one last time. "If you think of anything else that might be helpful, please let me know."

His jaw tight, "I'll keep that in mind."

As Lila walked out into the bright sunlight, her mind raced with possibilities. Graham's defensiveness, his evasive answers… it all pointed to a man with secrets.

As Lila walked away from Graham's gallery, a nagging feeling settled in her gut. His words kept replaying in her mind, each denial and deflection only fueling her suspicions.

Lila's footsteps echoed on the sidewalk as she made her way through the quaint streets of Willow Creek. The late afternoon sun cast long shadows across the path, dappling the ground with patches of light and dark. The air was thick with the scent of freshly cut grass.

She paused at the corner, fishing her phone out of her purse. Her fingers hovered over the keypad, considering her next move.

An idea formed, and she quickly dialed a number. "Hey, Sam," she said when the call connected. "Do you think there is anyway that we could get Graham

Whitaker's financials? Specifically, any transactions or communications with Evelyn Grey in the past year."

"Well I can't get his full financials, but I have access to Evelyn's business financials for the gallery now, since the police gave me back her computer. There should be a record of Graham's gallery financials also because of the merger. Would that work?"

"That's perfect, that's all I need."

Sam's voice crackled through the phone. "Give me a few hours. I'll see what I can dig up and send it your way."

"Thanks, Sam. I owe you one." Lila ended the call, a sense of purpose in her step. She was confident that Sam would find the records, so Lila could see if there was more to the merger than Graham was letting on.

As she walked through the bustling streets of downtown Willow Creek, her mind drifted back to her last conversation with Evelyn. The older woman had seemed stressed. At the time, Lila hadn't pressed for details.

Lila's regret twisted in her gut. She should have pushed Evelyn for more information on what had been bothering her. If she had, perhaps her friend would still be alive now.

She shook her head, banishing the thought. Dwelling on the past wouldn't help her solve the mystery of Evelyn's death. She needed to focus on the present, on following the clues, wherever they led.

And right now, those clues were pointing squarely at Graham Whitaker.

With determination, Lila quickened her pace, her mind already racing ahead to her next move.

Lila's key turned in the lock of her apartment, the familiar click a welcome sound after the tension-filled afternoon. As she stepped inside, the scent of lavender enveloped her, a comforting blend that usually calmed her nerves. But today, even the familiar surroundings couldn't ease the knot of anxiety in her stomach.

She dropped her bag on the worn leather armchair by the door, her eyes immediately drawn to her laptop. Her heart quickened as she crossed the room, hoping the records she'd been waiting for were there.

Lila settled onto her couch, balancing her laptop on her knees as she logged into her email. Her heart raced as she saw a new message from Samantha, with the subject line "Financial Records."

She clicked it open, her eyes scanning the contents rapidly:

"Lila,

I've attached what I could find on Graham's financial dealings with Evelyn's gallery over the past year. Take a look and let me know what you think.

Be careful,

Sam"

With nervous anticipation, she clicked to open the attached documents. Her eyes darted back and forth across the screen, taking in the columns of numbers and transaction details. At first glance, everything seemed normal - routine payments and transfers between the two galleries as they prepared for the merger.

As Lila pored over the financial records, her initial hopefulness slowly gave way to disappointment. Page after page of mundane transactions scrolled by - routine payments for advertising, transfers related to normal operating costs, even the occasional reimbursement for a business lunch. Everything seemed perfectly above board, each transaction meticulously documented and explained.

She leaned back against the couch cushions, rubbing her tired eyes. The soft glow of her laptop screen illuminated her furrowed brow as she tried to make sense of what she was seeing. Where were the suspicious transfers she had been so sure she'd find? The unexplained influxes of cash or questionable withdrawals?

Lila scrolled back to the top of the document, determined to go through it one more time. Perhaps she had missed something in her initial read. But as she carefully examined each line item, the truth became increasingly clear - there was nothing out of the ordinary in Graham's financial dealings with Evelyn's gallery.

The merger preparations were all there, laid out in black and white. Regular meetings, consultant fees, legal expenses - it all painted a picture of two galleries working towards a mutually beneficial partnership. Even the sudden halt in merger-related expenses lined up to when Evelyn had pulled out.

Lila sighed heavily, closing her laptop with a soft click. The financial records had been a dead end. There was nothing suspicious or incriminating in Graham's dealings with Evelyn's gallery. Everything was meticulously documented and above board.

She stood up and paced her small living room, frustration bubbling up inside her. She had been so sure that Graham was hiding something, that his financial records would reveal a motive for Evelyn's murder. But now she was back to square one.

CHAPTER 12

Samantha's hand shook as she reached for the door handle, the cool metal felt foreign under her fingertips. She took a deep breath as she looked at her reflection in the glass, steeling herself, and stepped inside.

Silence surrounded her. Samantha's eyes darted around the room, taking in the bare walls where vibrant paintings leaned waiting to be hung. Evelyn's presence lingered in every corner. But now, an eerie stillness had settled over the space like a shroud since Evelyn's death.

Samantha's gaze drifted to the scattered easels and canvases throughout the room. She could almost hear Evelyn's voice, warm and enthusiastic, as she described her vision for the upcoming exhibition. A lump formed in Samantha's throat.

As she ventured further into the gallery, memories flooded Samantha's mind. Evelyn's laughter echoing through the halls, the clink of champagne glasses at opening receptions, the hushed conversations between artists and admirers.

Samantha paused, her eyes drawn to the closed door of Evelyn's office. She swallowed hard, a shiver running down her spine. The last time she'd been there, she and Lila had discovered Evelyn's body, a sight that still haunted her dreams.

With a shaky breath, Samantha forced her feet forward, one step at a time. As she approached the office, the weight of her grief seemed to grow heavier with each passing moment. She reached out, her fingers grasping the doorknob.

Samantha turned the knob and pushed the door open, the hinges creaking. Freezing at the entrance, the office was just as Evelyn had left it. Papers were strewn across the desk, a novelty coffee mug of pens on top.

Samantha stepped into Evelyn's office, her heart heavy with the weight of her friend's absence. The room felt strangely still, as if even the air itself was mourning the loss of Evelyn's gardenia perfume. Samantha's gaze drifted to the desk, where countless hours had been spent planning art shows, discussing artists, and sharing dreams for the future.

With a deep breath, she settled into Evelyn's chair, the leather still bearing the floral scent of its former owner. Samantha reached for the stack of paperwork, her fingers trembling slightly as she began to sort through the documents. Ledgers, contracts, and proposals for upcoming shows—all bearing Evelyn's distinctive handwriting and meticulous attention to detail.

Samantha opened the bottom drawer of the desk, hoping to find a place to file away the sorted documents. As she reached inside, her fingers brushed against something unexpected—a plastic bag tucked behind and under a stack of old paperwork. Curiosity piqued, she carefully extracted the bag and placed it on the desk.

The bag was unmarked, giving no indication of its contents. Samantha hesitated for a moment, her heart racing with a mixture of anticipation and trepidation. Slowly, she opened the bag, revealing a series of letters addressed to Evelyn. The envelopes bore no return address, only Evelyn's name written in an unfamiliar hand.

Samantha's breath caught in her throat as she stared at the letters, a sense of unease creeping over her. She carefully extracted the letters from the plastic bag. The paper felt crisp beneath her fingers, the handwriting on the envelopes neat but unfamiliar. A part of her hesitated, not wanting to invade Evelyn's privacy.

But her curiosity got the better of her. Samantha took a deep breath and opened the first letter, her heart pounding in her chest. As her eyes scanned the words, a chill ran down her spine. The tone of the letter was harsh, accusatory, filled with a simmering rage that leapt off the page.

"Evelyn,

You think you can just ignore me? After everything we've been through?

I won't be erased so easily. You'll hear from me again soon. And next time, I won't be so polite."

It wasn't signed. Evelyn must have know who it was from. The rest of the letters were much the same, with phrases standing out as Sam continued to read

"You thought you could hide from your past, Evelyn," the letter began, "but the time has come for you to pay for your mistakes. You can't run forever."

Samantha's hands shook as she read on, the writer's words growing more menacing with each letter. "I know what you did, and I won't let you forget it. Your sins will catch up to you, and when they do, there will be no escape."

The letters were all unsigned, but the intensity of their hatred was palpable. Samantha's mind raced, trying to make sense of it all.

With a growing sense of unease, Samantha reached for the next letter, then the next. As she read the final lines of the last letter, Samantha felt a wave of dread wash over her. "The time for reckoning is near, Evelyn. You can't hide from the truth forever."

Samantha sat back in the chair, her mind reeling. These letters were no mere fan mail or business correspondence. There was a secret in Evelyn's past. Something that could potentially threaten them all.

"What had you gotten yourself into, Evelyn?" Samantha whispered. "What have you done?"

She knew, with a certainty that settled deep in her bones, that these letters held the key to unlocking the mystery of Evelyn's death. But the thought of what they might reveal, of the secrets they might uncover, filled her with fear.

Samantha's fingers trembled as she dialed Lila's number. The phone seemed to ring endlessly before Lila's voice, tinged with concern, finally answered. "Sam? What's wrong?"

"Lila, I found something. At the gallery. In Evelyn's office." Samantha's words tumbled out in a rush, her voice shaking. "I need you to come here. Right now."

"I'm on my way." Lila's response was immediate, no questions asked. She could hear the urgency, the barely contained panic, in Samantha's voice.

Lila's car came to a halt outside the gallery, leaving tire marks on the pavement. She burst through the unlocked door, heart racing as she rushed into the empty space.

"Sam?" she called out, her voice unnaturally loud in the stillness.

"In here." Samantha's voice drifted from Evelyn's office, weak and distant.

Lila moved quickly, her heart pounding in her chest. She stepped into the office and froze. Samantha was sitting at Evelyn's desk, her face pale, her hands resting on a stack of papers. The air in the room felt heavy, weighted with tension.

"What is it? What did you find?" Lila approached slowly, as if moving too quickly might shatter the fragile calm.

Wordlessly, Samantha held out the papers. Lila took them, her eyes scanning the first lines. And then she began to read, her breath catching in her throat.

She looked up, her eyes meeting Samantha's. In that moment, a silent understanding passed between them. This had to be related to what had happened to Evelyn.

Lila's mind raced as she paced the office, reading the letters clutched tightly in her hand. Samantha sat at Evelyn's desk, her brow furrowed with worry.

"I don't understand," Samantha said, her voice barely above a whisper. "Why wouldn't Evelyn tell anyone about these letters? Why would she keep something like this to herself?"

Lila paused, turning to face her friend. "Maybe she didn't take the threats seriously. You said they were hidden at the bottom of the desk. Or maybe she didn't want to worry anyone."

"But these letters... they're so terrifying. How could she not take them seriously?"

"I don't know, Sam. She was so strong and confident, maybe she thought she could handle it on her own. Maybe she knew who was sending them and wanted to deal with it herself."

Samantha shook her head, her eyes glistening with unshed tears. "I just can't believe she wouldn't tell us. We were her friends. We could have helped her."

Lila sighed, sinking into the chair opposite Samantha. "I know. But we can't change the past. All we can do now is try to find out who did this."

She glanced down at the letters again, her mind whirling with possibilities. Julian's words echoed in her head, his theory about someone from Evelyn's past being the culprit.

"You know," she said slowly, "this lines up with what Julian said. About Evelyn having enemies from her past."

Samantha's eyes widened. "You think this could be one of them?"

"It's possible. Whoever sent these letters clearly had a grudge against Evelyn. And if they're not one of our current suspects…"

"Then it could be someone we haven't even considered yet," Samantha finished, her voice trembling slightly.

Lila nodded, her mind racing with the implications. She took a deep breath, realizing she needed to fill Samantha in on her own findings - or lack thereof.

"Sam, I should tell you… I went through those financial records you sent me earlier," Lila began, her voice tinged with disappointment. "I was so sure we'd find something suspicious in Graham's dealings with Evelyn, but…"

She trailed off, shaking her head. Samantha leaned forward, her brow furrowed. "But what? What did you find?"

"Nothing. It's all perfectly above board. The merger preparations, the routine payments, even the sudden halt when Evelyn pulled out - it's all there, meticulously documented. There's nothing suspicious about Graham's financial dealings with Evelyn's gallery."

Samantha's eyes widened in surprise. "Really, so where does that leave us? If Graham's financials check out…"

"It means we might have been looking in the wrong direction all along," Lila finished, her gaze drifting back to the threatening letters on the desk. "These letters... they could be the key to everything."

Samantha nodded, her expression resolute despite the fear that lingered in her eyes. "We should call Detective Reed," she said, "He needs to know about this."

Lila reached into her pocket and pulled out her phone. As she scrolled through her contacts, her mind continued to race, piecing together the fragments of information they had gathered so far. Evelyn's murder, the threatening letters, Julian's suspicions about a figure from Evelyn's past. Things that Marcus might ask about.

Lila's fingers hovered over her phone, a heavy silence filling the room. She glanced at Samantha, who nodded encouragingly.

With a deep breath, she dialed Marcus's number, her heart pounding in her chest as she waited for him to pick up.

"Detective Reed," he answered, his voice crisp and businesslike.

"Marcus, it's Lila. I'm at the gallery with Samantha. We found something... something important."

There was a pause on the other end of the line, and Lila could almost picture Marcus's skeptical expression. "What kind of something?"

"Letters. Threatening letters, addressed to Evelyn. They talk about her paying for her mistakes. Marcus, I think whoever wrote these might be responsible for her death."

Another pause, longer this time. Lila's palms were sweating, and she wiped them on her jeans, trying to keep her voice steady.

"Read them to me," Marcus said finally, his tone grave.

Lila took a shaky breath and began to read, the words burning like acid on her tongue. When she finished, there was a long silence on the other end of the line.

But then he spoke, his voice tight with controlled urgency. "Stay where you are. I'm coming to collect the letters. Don't touch anything else, and don't leave until I get there. Understand?"

Lila nodded, forgetting for a moment that he couldn't see her. "Yes. We'll be here."

She hung up, her hand trembling as she lowered the phone. Samantha looked at her expectantly, hope and fear warring in her eyes.

"He's coming," Lila said, her voice sounding distant to her own ears. "He wants us to wait here."

Samantha nodded, wrapping her arms around herself as if to ward off a chill.

The minutes ticked by, each one an eternity. Lila paced the office. She paused at Evelyn's desk, her fingers tracing the polished wood.

The sound of the gallery door opening made them both jump. Lila's heart raced as footsteps approached. A moment later, Marcus appeared in the doorway.

"Marcus," Lila nodded, gesturing to the desk. "They were hidden in the bottom drawer. I hate to say it, but we touched all of them. We wanted to make sure they were all relevant."

Marcus sighed as he snapped on a pair of gloves and carefully picked up the letters, his eyes scanning the contents.

The detective slipped the letters into an evidence bag. "We'll analyze these at the lab. See if we can find any fingerprints or DNA." He fixed Lila with a stern look. "In the meantime, I need you to stay out of the investigation. Leave this to the professionals."

Lila bristled at the dismissal, but she forced herself to nod. "Of course. We found theses by accident." She couldn't help but feel a little guilty for lying to him.

Marcus softened slightly, his eyes sympathetic. "I know. But the best way you can help is by letting us do our job." He tucked the evidence bag under his arm and headed for the door. "Be careful Lila. Stay out of this."

As the detective's footsteps faded away, Lila turned to Samantha, her eyes blazing with determination. "We're not giving up," she said, her voice low and fierce.

Samantha nodded, her own resolve hardening.

CHAPTER 13

The bell above the diner door chimed, signaling Lila's arrival. She scanned the retro booths and speckled Formica counters, her fingers nervously twisting a paint-splattered scarf. Samantha waved from a corner table, a steaming mug already cradled in her other hand.

Sliding into the seat across from her friend, Lila exhaled heavily. "I can't stop thinking about those letters, Sam. Who would've threatened Evelyn like that?"

Samantha shook her head, concern etched on her face. "I don't know. But inviting Maxine...are we sure that's a good idea? She doesn't exactly strike me as a friendly person."

Lila bit her lip, uncertainty clouding her blue eyes. "She knew Evelyn long before we did. If anyone has insights into her past, it's Maxine." She fidgeted with her phone, glancing at the door every few seconds.

"Fine, but for now lets hold off on telling her about the letters we found for." Sam suggested. "Just a little bit longer."

Lila nodded her agreement.

Minutes ticked by in tense silence until the bell chimed again. Maxine strode in, her vibrant hair tousled, a leather jacket hugging her slim frame. Gone was the aloof demeanor from their previous encounters. She greeted them with a warm smile as she approached the table.

"Lila, Samantha, I'm glad we could meet." Maxine slid into the booth, genuine interest sparkling in her eyes. "I've been doing a lot of digging about Evelyn...I think I may have come up with a few promising leads."

Lila blinked in surprise, taken aback by Maxine's shifted attitude. Perhaps grief had softened her edges. She cleared her throat. "We appreciate that, Maxine. Truly. Evelyn's death has left us with so many questions."

Maxine nodded, her expression somber. "I can only imagine." She leaned forward, lowering her voice. "I might know where to start looking for answers."

Lila's heartbeat quickened. Finally, they might have a lead into Evelyn's past. She exchanged a glance with

Samantha, who still looked hesitant. But Lila's instincts told her to trust Maxine's sincerity.

"What did you find out," Lila urged, her curiosity overpowering any lingering doubts.

Maxine leaned back, her fingers drumming on the table as she gathered her thoughts. "It all started about ten years ago," she began, her voice low and conspiratorial. "There was this wealthy collector, a real high-roller in the art world. He approached Evelyn with an offer to buy a series of paintings from one of her most promising artists. It would have been a career-defining sale for him."

Lila leaned in, hanging on to every word. "So what happened? Did the sale go through?"

Maxine shook her head, a shadow crossing her face. "No. At the last minute, Evelyn pulled out. She refused to sell, even though it meant losing a massive commission for both her and the artist."

Lila furrowed her brow. "That doesn't sound like Evelyn. She was always so supportive of her artists' success. What made her back out?"

Maxine sighed, running a hand through her vibrant hair. "That's the thing. Evelyn never gave a clear explanation, not even to the artist. It caused a huge rift between them. The artist ended up leaving the gallery, his career took a nosedive after that."

Samantha piped up, her voice tinged with concern. "Do you think this could be related to Evelyn's death?"

Maxine paused, her eyes distant as she seemed to be sifting through memories. "It's possible. The whole situation was swept under the rug. Evelyn never spoke about it openly, not even to her closest friends."

"I've never heard the story," Lila agreed. She sat back, her mind churning with unanswered questions. "Who was the artist? The one whose work Evelyn refused to sell?"

Maxine's lips twisted into a rueful smile. "That's the thing. I don't know. Evelyn always refused to give her name. But I'll keep digging. I have more contacts that haven't gotten back to me yet."

The waitress arrived with their orders, momentarily interrupting the flow of conversation. Lila wrapped her hands around her steaming mug of coffee, the warmth grounding her as she processed Maxine's revelations.

"So, what happened between you and Evelyn," Lila probed, her eyes locked on Maxine. "Why have we never seen you before?"

Maxine sighed, stirring her tea absentmindedly. "It was early in my career. I was young, ambitious, and maybe a bit naïve. Evelyn and I had been working on my first show—my first big break."

She paused, taking a sip of her tea before continued. "I wanted a larger percentage of the sales. Evelyn insisted on sticking to the industry standard. We argued, things got heated, and I walked away from the deal."

Lila nodded. She had been shocked by the industry commissions when she first heard them too. She could picture the scene vividly—two strong-willed women, both passionate about their art, clashing over money and pride.

"And after that?" Samantha chimed in, her curiosity kicking in.

Maxine shrugged. "We didn't speak for years. I focused on my own career in the city, determined to prove I could make it without her. But Evelyn... she had a way of getting under your skin. Even when we weren't speaking, I couldn't stop thinking about her."

Lila felt a pang of empathy. She knew all too well the complexities of a mentor-mentee relationship, the blurred lines between admiration and resentment.

Lila leaned forward, her voice soft with understanding. "Evelyn had that effect on people. She could be both inspiring and infuriating, often at the same time."

"Who was the collector?" Sam asked, going back to the lead Maxine had.

Maxine leaned forward, her eyes darting around the diner as if checking for eavesdroppers. "The art collector, I can't remember his name right now, but I'll get it too you. But that's not the most interesting thing I found out. I've heard rumors about forgeries."

Sam gasped, "that can't be true. I've worked for Evelyn for years and there has never been any hint of a forgery."

Lila frowned, her mind racing with the implications of Maxine's words. "Forgeries? Are you sure? Evelyn was always so meticulous about the authenticity of the works in her gallery."

Maxine nodded grimly. "I thought the same. But these rumors have been circulating in certain circles. Whispers about a master forger who managed to slip a few pieces past Evelyn's discerning eye."

Lila felt a chill run down her spine. The idea of forgeries infiltrating Evelyn's gallery seemed unfathomable. She had always trusted her mentor's judgment implicitly.

"But who would do such a thing?" Lila asked, her voice barely above a whisper.

Maxine nodded, her expression darkening. "It was years ago, but then there were whispers that Evelyn had gotten involved with a forgery ring. Allegedly, they were creating near-perfect replicas of famous works and selling them to unsuspecting collectors."

Samantha's eyebrows shot up. "No, Evelyn would never do something like that."

"That's what she said," Maxine clarified. "But some people in the art world started giving her the side-eye. Wondering if maybe she wasn't as squeaky clean as she appeared."

Lila's mind raced with the implications. If Evelyn had been involved with forgeries, it could have created some dangerous enemies.

She glanced at Samantha, silently communicating her desire to dig deeper. Her friend gave a subtle nod, a silent agreement to follow this lead wherever it took them.

Maxine sat back in her chair, looking drained from the weight of her revelations. "That's all I know. I wish I could give you more, but Evelyn... she played her cards close to the chest, but I will keep looking.'"

Lila reached across the table, giving Maxine's hand a reassured squeeze. "You've given us more than enough to work with. Thank you, Maxine. Truly."

Lila straightened her shoulders, her eyes alight with determination. "Okay, here's the plan. Maxine, if you could keep looking into the people who might know more about Evelyn's dealings with potential forgeries, I'll keep looking into Graham and other possible suspects in Willow Creek."

Maxine nodded, already pulling out her phone. "Consider it done."

As they gathered their belongings and prepared to leave, Lila couldn't help but feel a glimmer of hope. With each new piece of information, they were inching closer to the truth.

Maxine stood from the table and looked down and Samantha and Lila. Her expression earnest. "I know we just met and don't really know each other very well, but I want you to know that I'm here for you both. I'll do everything I can to help find out what happened to Evelyn."

Lila felt a lump form in her throat, touched by Maxine's sincerity. She nodded, not trusting herself to speak. As Maxine slipped out the door, Lila exchanged a glance with Samantha.

Samantha shifted her weight, her brow furrowed. "What about the threatening letters? I still think we should follow up with Marcus, see if he's found out anything new."

Lila hesitated, torn between her desire to pursue the new leads or to follow up about the letters. "You're right, Sam. We can't ignore the letters. How about this—you touch base with Marcus, and I'll see if I can find out more about Graham since Maxine is looking into the forgery angle. We'll cover more ground that way."

Samantha's shoulders relaxed, a small smile tugging at her lips. "Sounds like a plan. I'll call Marcus as soon as I get back to the gallery."

Lila and Samantha lingered at the table, both lost in thought. The diner bustled around them, the clatter of dishes and hum of conversation a stark contrast to the heavy silence that had settled over their booth.

Samantha was the first to break the stillness. "Do you really think Evelyn could have been involved in something like that? Forgeries, I mean." Her voice was hesitant.

Lila sighed, her fingers tracing the rim of her coffee mug. "I don't know, Sam. It's hard to imagine Evelyn being involved in anything shady. She was always so principled, so passionate about the integrity of the art world."

Samantha nodded, her expression pensive. "But if there's even a shred of truth to these rumors, we owe it to Evelyn to find out. She does not deserve to have her reputation ruined over nothing."

Lila's mind churned with the weight of their new-found knowledge as they left the diner. The idea that Evelyn could have been involved in a forgery ring seemed unfathomable.

Chapter 14

Lila's fingers twitched restlessly as she rearranged her paints, her mind far from the usual peace she found in her studio. The phone rang, shattering her trance. She snatched it up, hoping for good news.

"Sam, do you have an update from Marcus about those letters," Lila said, her words tumbling out in a rush.

Samantha's sigh crackled through the speaker. "I'm sorry, Lila. I haven't had a chance to follow up with him yet. I've been swamped trying to reschedule the gallery show and clear out Evelyn's office." Frustration bled into her normally calm voice.

"That's ok Sam. I'm not getting much work done here. I'll just head over to the police station myself. I'll fill Marcus in on what we heard from Maxine about those rumors, and see if he's made any progress with the letters."

"Lila, are you sure that's a good idea? Wouldn't a phone call be better." Concern laced Samantha's words.

"I don't mind. We need answers, and it's harder for Marcus to brush me off in person." Lila's jaw clenched, her fingers gripping the phone tightly.

Samantha's hesitation was palpable, even through the phone line. "Okay, but be careful. Don't push him too hard. The last thing we need is to have the police shut us out completely."

"I'll handle Marcus. Don't worry." Lila ended the call before Samantha could argue further. With a deep breath, Lila strode out of her studio. One way or another, she would get the truth.

As she approached her car, a flash of white caught her eye. Her heart skipped a beat as she realized what it was - another photograph, tucked neatly under her windshield wiper. With trembling fingers, she plucked it free, her breath catching in her throat as she took in the image.

It was a crisp, high-resolution shot of her and Samantha at the diner, taken just a few hours ago. The angle suggested it had been taken from across the street, capturing their intense conversation. Lila's face was clearly visible, her expression a mix of concern and determination. Samantha's back was to the camera, but her tense posture was clear.

Lila's hands shook as she clutched the photograph, her heart pounding in her chest. She glanced around wildly, searching for any sign of the mysterious photographer, but the street was empty. With a shuddering breath, she shoved the photo into her bag and slid into her car, fumbling with the keys as she started the engine.

As Lila drove towards the police station, the streets of Willow Creek seemed different now, tinged with an air of menace she'd never felt before. Lila's gaze darted constantly to her rearview mirror, searching for any sign of a tail. But the traffic behind her remained normal - a mix of locals running errands and the occasional tourist.

As she approached the police station, the imposing brick building loomed before her, its windows gleaming in the late afternoon sun. Lila pulled into the parking lot, the crunch of gravel under her tires seeming unnaturally loud in the quiet air. She chose a spot near the entrance, wanting to minimize her time outside where she felt exposed.

Taking a deep breath, Lila cut the engine and sat for a moment, gathering her courage. The photograph burned in her bag, a tangible reminder of the danger she faced. But she couldn't turn back now. She had come too far, uncovered too much.

With a determined set to her jaw, Lila stepped out of the car. The crisp autumn air nipped at her cheeks as she strode towards the station's entrance. The front desk clerk, a woman with a tight bun and a no-nonsense demeanor, glanced up as Lila entered. Recognition flickered in her eyes, followed by a wary look.

"Ms. Montgomery. Here to see Detective Reed?" The clerk's tone held a hint of exasperation.

Lila nodded, her resolve unwavering. "Yes. It's urgent."

The clerk sighed, gesturing down one of the hallways behind her. "His office is down that hallway, fourth door on the left."

Lila murmured a quick thanks and strode past the desk. The hallway stretched before her, the fluorescent lights casting a harsh glare. She counted the doors until she reached Marcus's office.

As she approached, Lila noticed the door was slightly ajar. Muffled voices filtered through the gap, and she caught a glimpse of Marcus hunched over his desk, buried in paperwork while talking on the phone.

She rapped her knuckles against the door, pushing it open without waiting for a response.

Marcus's head snapped up, his eyes widening in surprise. "I'll have to call you back," Marcus said as he disconnected the phone. "Lila? What are you doing here?" He set down his pen, leaning back in his chair. His tone was more weary than welcoming.

Lila stood in the doorway, her hand still on the knob. "We need to talk, Marcus. About the case."

Marcus's brow furrowed. "Once again Lila, this is an active investigation. I can't have civilians interfering."

"I'm not interfering." Lila stepped into the office, closing the door behind her with a firm click. "I'm trying to help. Samantha and I have information that could be vital to solving Evelyn's murder."

Marcus's jaw tightened. "Lila, I appreciate your concern, but you need to let me handle this. You're not a detective."

Lila bristled at his dismissive tone. She knew he was just doing his job, but his stubborn refusal to listen was infuriating. "No, I'm not. But Sam and I knew Evelyn better than anyone. And I'm not going to sit by and watch her killer go free because of bureaucratic red tape."

She moved closer to the desk, her eyes locked on Marcus's. "Please, just hear me out. Five minutes, that's all I ask."

Marcus held her gaze for a long moment, his expression unreadable. Finally, he sighed, gesturing to the chair across from his desk. "Fine. Five minutes. But I can't promise anything."

Lila sank into the chair, her heart pounding. She had one chance to convince Marcus. One chance to steer the investigation in the right direction. She took a deep breath, gathering her thoughts.

Lila leaned forward, her voice urgent. "Maxine told us that Evelyn may have had a history of dealing with forgeries, but I don't believe that. She also said that Evelyn had strained relationships with some art collectors who Evelyn refused to sell too. But I don't have any names."

Marcus's brow furrowed. "We're aware of those rumors, but that's all they are, rumors."

"Maybe not. It could give us a motive." Lila's mind raced, piecing together the fragments of information.

"It's a possibility," Marcus conceded, "but we can't jump to conclusions based on rumors and speculation. You don't have any names. How am I supposed to find something concrete?"

Lila shook her head, frustrated. "It's more than that. Maxine said Evelyn was worried. She thought someone from her past might be coming after her."

Marcus's eyes narrowed. "Did Maxine give any specifics? Names, dates, anything concrete?"

"No, but..." Lila hesitated, realizing how flimsy the information sounded out loud. "Look, I know it's not much to go on, but it's a lead. We should be looking into Evelyn's past, trying to find out who might have had a grudge against her."

Marcus sighed, rubbing his temple. "Lila, I understand your frustration, but you have to trust me. We're already looking into every angle, including Evelyn's past. But these things take time. We can't rush the investigation based on hearsay and conjecture."

Lila bit her lip, fighting back a surge of anger. She knew Marcus was just doing his job, but his dismissal of her concerns stung. "So, what, you expect me to just sit back and do nothing?"

"I expect you to let me handle it." Marcus's tone was firm, leaving no room for argument. "I know you want answers, but you need to stay out of this. For your own safety, and for the integrity of the investigation."

Lila stared at him, her eyes blazing with defiance. She wanted to argue, to make him see how important this was to her. But something in his expression made her pause. Beneath the irritation and impatience, she saw a flicker of genuine concern.

Lila took a deep breath, her fingers tightening around the strap of her bag. She could feel the weight of the photographs inside, pressing against her side like a guilty secret. The words caught in her throat, but she forced them out.

"Marcus, there's something else. Something I haven't told you."

His eyebrows raised, curiosity replacing the frustration in his eyes. "Go on."

Lila hesitated slightly before she reached into her bag, pulling out the two photographs. She laid them on Marcus's desk, the glossy surfaces catching the harsh fluorescent light.

"These were left for me. The first one appeared on my studio door a few days ago, and the second..." She swallowed hard. "The second was on my car windshield just before I came here."

Marcus leaned forward, his eyes scanning the images with practiced efficiency. The first photo of Lila,

Samantha, and Julian at the diner, the second of Lila and Samantha.

Marcus's expression darkened as he studied the photographs. His jaw clenched, a muscle twitching beneath the skin. "Why didn't you tell me about these sooner?" His voice was low, controlled, but Lila could hear the anger simmering beneath the surface.

Lila shifted in her seat, guilt gnawing at her insides. "I... I didn't want to worry you. I thought maybe it was nothing, just someone trying to scare me off the investigation."

Marcus leaned forward, his voice softening slightly. "Lila, I know you loved Evelyn. But you have to let the police do their job. We'll find her killer, I promise you that. But you need to trust the process, and trust me."

Lila swallowed hard, torn between her desire for justice and the realization that Marcus was right. She couldn't risk compromising the investigation, no matter how badly she wanted answers.

"Okay," she said finally, her voice barely above a whisper. "I'll back off. But you have to keep me informed. I need to know what's happening."

Marcus nodded, a hint of relief in his eyes. "I will. I promise."

Lila's shoulders sagged with a mixture of defeat and exhaustion.

"Just...find whoever did this. For Evelyn."

Marcus met her gaze, his expression solemn. "I will. You have my word."

Marcus sighed, some of the tension leaving his shoulders. "I know you mean well, Lila. But you have to understand the position you're putting yourself in."

Lila swallowed hard, the reality of the situation hitting her like a punch to the gut. She had been so focused on finding answers, on getting justice for Evelyn, that she hadn't fully considered the risks.

Lila squared her shoulders, meeting Marcus' gaze head-on. "I understand the risks."

"I don't think you do." Marcus held her gaze for a long moment, a flicker of defeat mingling with the frustration in his eyes. Finally, he nodded. "I can't stop you from looking into this on your own time. But I'm warning you, be careful. Don't do anything reckless, and don't interfere with official police business."

Lila nodded, a sense of resolve settling over her. "I'll be careful."

With that, she stood and walked out of Marcus' office, her head held high.

Lila stepped out into the bright sunlight and walked towards her car, her steps heavy with the weight of her thoughts. As she reached for the door handle, her phone buzzed in her pocket. She pulled it out, seeing Samantha's name on the screen.

"Hey, Sam," Lila answered, her voice weary.

"Lila, how did it go with Marcus? Did you tell him about what Maxine said?" Samantha's voice was eager, expectant.

Lila sighed, leaning against her car. "I did, but he didn't seem to think it was important. He already knew about Evelyn's past issues."

"What? That was it?"

Lila hesitated, Marcus's warning ringing in her ears. She didn't want to worry Samantha, but she also needed to confide in someone.

Lila took a deep breath, her fingers tightening around the phone. "There's more, Sam. I... I showed Marcus the photographs."

"Photographs? What photographs?" Samantha's voice was laced with confusion and concern.

Lila glanced around the parking lot, suddenly feeling exposed. She lowered her voice, cupping her hand around the phone. "Someone's been following us, Sam. Taking pictures. The first one showed up on my studio door a few days ago - it was of us and Julian at the diner. And today... there was another one. On my car windshield. It was from our meeting with Maxine, earlier in the day."

Samantha gasped, the sound sharp in Lila's ear. "Oh my God, Lila. Why didn't you tell me?"

Guilt twisted in Lila's stomach. "I didn't want to worry you. I thought... I don't know what I thought. That maybe it was nothing, just someone trying to scare us off."

Samantha's sharp intake of breath crackled through the line. "Oh my God, Lila. Did Marcus say anything about who might be doing this?"

Lila shook her head, forgetting for a moment that Samantha couldn't see her. "He doesn't know. But he was... concerned. He made me promise to back off the investigation."

"And did you? Promise, I mean?" Samantha's voice was hesitant.

"I think," she said slowly, "we need to stop digging. That we need to let the police handle it."

"Are you sure?" Samantha asked, "I can keep looking into Evelyn's past dealings, see if I can find any leads."

Lila hesitated, torn between her promise to Marcus and her burning need for answers. "No," she said finally, her voice heavy with resignation. "We can't risk it, Sam. If we keep pushing, it could jeopardize the whole investigation. Marcus was pretty clear about that."

Samantha sighed. "Okay, if that's what you think is best. But Lila, I'm here for you. Don't forget that."

Lila felt a surge of gratitude. "I know, Sam. Thank you."

Lila ended the call, slipping her phone back into her pocket. She took one last look at the police station, her resolve hardening. She would let Marcus handle the investigation from here on out.

CHAPTER 15

L ila took a deep breath as she opened the gallery door the following week. The cool metal of the handle felt heavy beneath her fingertips, a physical weight to match the emotional one settling in her chest.

She stepped inside, the familiar scent of paint and canvas enveloping her. But something was different. The trace of Evelyn's floral scent that was a staple of her gallery was gone. Lila paused, clearing the tears from her eyes. Samantha was already there, her petite frame adjusting one of the paintings on the wall as she directed the rest of the gallery staff.

"Morning, Sam," Lila said, her voice sounding too quite in the chaos.

Samantha looked up, offering a small smile that didn't quite reach her eyes. "Hey, Lila. Rough night?"

Lila shrugged, setting her bag down and shrugging off her jacket. "You could say that."

Samantha's brow furrowed with concern as she set down the painting she'd been adjusting. She crossed the room, her footsteps echoing softly on the polished wood floor. "Why was it rough? What's going on?"

"I can't stop thinking about those photographs," Lila admitted, her voice barely above a whisper. "It's like... I can feel someone watching me, all the time. Even when I'm alone."

She met Samantha in the middle of the room, as the gallery staff worked around them.

Samantha nodded sympathetically, her eyes scanning the gallery. "I know what you mean. It's unsettling, to say the least." She gestured around the room. "But maybe focusing on the show will help take our minds off things for a while."

Lila nodded, forcing herself to take in the chaos surrounding them. The gallery was a whirlwind of activity, a stark contrast to the eerie stillness of the past few weeks.

"You're right," Lila agreed, forcing a smile.

As Lila moved through the gallery, she saw Adrian emerge from the back room, his dark hair tousled and his jaw set. He nodded at Lila, a brief acknowledgment before turning his attention to a large abstract painting. Lila watched him work, noting the tension in his shoulders and the furrow of his brow.

Lila tried to focus on the task at hand, arranging and rearranging her pieces for the show. But her mind kept drifting, replaying her discussion with Marcus. His words echoed in her head, his warning and her promise.

She glanced at Adrian again. While Lila still believed that Adrian didn't kill Evelyn, she was beginning to wonder if he knew more than he was letting on. The thought made her stomach twist. She wanted to trust him, but the shadows in his eyes gave her pause.

She needed to focus.

She picked up a small painting from an easel, turning it over in her hands. The weight of it grounded her, pulling her back to the present. She had a job to do, a show to put on. The rest would have to wait.

Lila sat the easel down and moved to her next painting, a large abstract piece that demanded attention. As she adjusted its position on the wall, her ears caught the murmur of a conversation nearby. She glanced over her shoulder, spotting Adrian talking quietly with one of the gallery assistants, a young man named Ethan.

At first, their words were too low to make out. But as Lila worked, she found herself inching closer, her curiosity pulling her in like a magnet.

"...can't believe it happened," Ethan said, his voice tinged with disbelief. "I mean, who would want to hurt Evelyn?"

Adrian shook his head, his expression grim. "I don't know. It doesn't make sense."

Lila's heart quickened. They were talking about the murder. She shifted slightly, hiding behind a painting, pretending to study it while straining to hear more.

"You know," Ethan said, his tone dropping to a conspiratorial whisper, "I think I saw something that night. Something strange."

Adrian's brows furrowed. "What do you mean?"

"Well, I was leaving the gallery late, after we'd finished setting up for the show. And I could've sworn I saw Graham Whitaker outside, just across the street."

Lila nearly dropped the painting. Graham? But he'd told her he was out of town that night, having dinner with a friend.

She risked a glance at Adrian, saw the surprise flicker across his face. "Are you sure it was him?" he asked.

Ethan nodded. "Pretty sure. I mean, it was dark, but I recognized his coat. That fancy one he always wears."

Lila's mind raced. If Ethan was right, it meant Graham had lied about his whereabouts.

She realized her hands were shaking, her thoughts spinning. Had Graham lied to her?

Lila's instincts screamed at her to act, to confront Graham and demand the truth. But her promise to Marcus' echoed in her head, a counterpoint to her racing thoughts.

She closed her eyes, torn between the pull of the mystery and her promise to Marcus. In that moment, standing with the art in Evelyn's gallery, Lila felt the weight of her friend's absence like a physical ache.

Adrian's voice cut through Lila's thoughts. "I'm sure it was just a mistake, Ethan. Graham told me he was in Oakwood Valley having dinner with a friend."

Lila caught the nervous edge in Adrian's tone, the way his eyes darted away from the assistant's questioning gaze. She stepped out from behind the painting, her presence startling both men.

"Lila, I didn't see you there," Adrian said, his voice strained.

"Sorry, I didn't mean to eavesdrop. But I couldn't help overhearing…" She let the sentence hang, her eyes searching Adrian's face.

He shifted uncomfortably, his hands fidgeting at his sides. "It's nothing, really. Just a misunderstanding."

But Lila could see the doubt in his eyes, the way his brow furrowed as he glanced at Ethan. The assistant looked between them, clearly sensing the tension.

"I should get back to work," Ethan said, excusing himself with a nod.

As he walked away, Lila turned to Adrian, her voice low. "What's going on, Adrian? Why would Graham lie about where he was that night?"

Adrian ran a hand through his hair, his eyes darting around the gallery. "I don't know, Lila. Maybe he had a reason. Maybe it's not what it seems."

But Lila could hear the uncertainty in his words. She stepped closer, her gaze intense.

"Adrian, if you know something, you need to tell me. This could be important."

He met her eyes then, and Lila saw the conflict there, the struggle between loyalty and truth. "I don't know anything for sure. Graham told me he was in Oakwood Valley. But if Graham was here that night…"

He trailed off, the implication clear. Lila's heart raced, her mind whirling with possibilities. She knew she needed to talk to Graham again, to confront him with what she'd learned.

But Marcus' warning was still fresh in her mind. She couldn't shake the feeling that she was walking into something dangerous, something she might not be prepared for.

She had to talk to Graham. Had to figure out the truth.

Lila squared her shoulders, her resolve hardening. She turned to Adrian, her voice steady.

"I'm going to talk to him."

Adrian looked at her, his expression a mix of concern and admiration. "Be careful, Lila. You don't know what you're getting into."

She nodded, the weight of his words settling on her shoulders. And Lila would stop at nothing to find the truth.

Lila's heart raced as she moved through the gallery on the way to the exit, her mind a whirlwind of thoughts and emotions. The revelation about Graham's potential deceit had shaken her.

She emerged into the late morning air, determined. She needed to do this.

But even as the thought crossed her mind, Marcus' warning resurfaced, his words a haunting reminder of the dangers that lay ahead.

"Stay out of it, Lila. For your own safety, and for the integrity of the investigation."

Her hand lingered over the car door handle, her mind racing with doubt. Evelyn's killer deserves to be brought to justice.

With a deep breath, Lila climbed into her car, the engine roaring to life beneath her. She pulled out of the parking lot, her destination clear in her mind.

Graham's gallery.

Lila's thoughts raced, pieces of the puzzle clicking into place with each passing mile. Graham's lie about his whereabouts, Adrian's reaction to the news, the strange tension that had hung between them all since Evelyn's death.

It all pointed to something deeper, something sinister lurking beneath the surface.

Lila's grip tightened on the steering wheel, her knuckles turning white with the force of her resolve. She uttered an apology to herself. "I'm sorry, Marcus. But I have to do this."

With a final glance in the rearview mirror, Lila pressed down on the accelerator and the car surged forward.

CHAPTER 16

As Lila approached Graham's gallery, her heart pounding in her chest, she slowed her car to a crawl. The morning sun glinted in the windows on the street. Her eyes scanned the familiar façade of Graham's gallery, taking in the elegant signage and the large display windows.

But something was off. The gallery, usually a hub of activity at this hour, stood eerily still. The lights were dimmed, and there was no sign of movement inside. Lila's brow furrowed as she pulled up alongside the curb, her eyes never leaving the darkened windows.

She put the car in park, her hand hovering over the door handle. Part of her wanted to march right up to the gallery, to pound on the door until Graham appeared and answered her questions. But another part, the more cautious side, held her back.

She drummed her fingers against the steering wheel, weighing her options. The adrenaline that had fueled her drive was fading, leaving her feeling drained and uncertain. With a sigh, Lila decided to regroup and gather her thoughts.

Lila's eyes drifted across the street, landing on the coffee shop. The warm glow from its windows beckoned invitingly. With a final glance at Graham's darkened gallery, Lila stepped out of her car. The scent of freshly ground coffee beans and warm pastries wafted out as she pushed open the door.

As she moved towards the counter, a flash of vibrant color caught Lila's attention. Her breath caught in her throat as she recognized the multicolored hair belonging to Maxine. The artist was seated at a small table by the window, her back to the door. Maxine's posture was hunched, her focus entirely on the phone at her ear.

Lila joined the line of customers, her eyes darting to the corner where Maxine sat, still engrossed in her phone call. Lila tensed as she started to hear the conversation over the noise of the coffee shop, catching only snippets of hushed words.

"...they'll catch on if we're not careful..." Maxine's voice was low, urgent.

Lila's brow furrowed.

"...I don't think she made it to the feds with any information..." Maxine's eyes flickered around the room, never landing on Lila.

A chill ran down Lila's spine.

Memories of Julian's warning echoed in her mind. "I wouldn't be surprised if it was an artist she disagreed with or someone holding a long standing grudge." Lila had brushed it off then, but now...

She studied Maxine's tense posture, the way her fingers gripped the phone like a lifeline.

Lila's heart stopped as doubt crept in. She thought back to their last conversation, how Maxine had deflected questions about her falling out with Evelyn.

The line inched forward, but Lila barely noticed. Her mind spun with possibilities, each more unsettling than the last.

She watched as Maxine ended the call, her movements sharp and hurried. Lila's stomach churned at the thought of Evelyn involved in something illegal. If that was the case, could Maxine be a part of it as well?

The barista's voice jolted her back to the present. "Next in line, please!"

Lila stepped forward, her decision made. She needed more information before she confronted Maxine.

She ordered her usual mocha, her voice steady despite the turmoil within.

As she waited for her drink, Lila's mind raced. Graham and Maxine, there were now two people that might have information. And one was definitely lying. She knew she couldn't ignore either lead, but the weight of her suspicions pulled her in different directions.

Lila decided, she'd start with Graham. Grabbing her mocha from the counter, Lila's resolve hardened, a steely determination that cut through the doubt and confusion.

Her mocha clutched tightly in her hand, Lila slipped out of the coffee shop, staying out of Maxine's sight. The gallery down the street was now open, looming before her. She took a deep breath, steeling herself for the confrontation ahead.

Chapter 17

The gallery door swung open with a gentle chime, announcing Lila's entrance into the pristine white space.

A few well-dressed patrons meandered through the paintings, their hushed conversations punctuating the tranquil atmosphere. Lila scanned the room. She spotted Graham near the back of the gallery, his tall frame bent over a crate of paintings. He looked up as she approached, surprise flickering across his face before settling into a guarded expression.

"Lila," he greeted her, his tone even. "I wasn't expecting to see you again so soon."

Lila met his gaze steadily. "I know our last few conversations were tense, Graham, but something's come up. I spoke with one of Evelyn's assistants, and they claimed you were seen near her gallery the night of the murder." She paused, letting her words hang in the air between them. "You told me you were in Oakwood Valley having dinner with a friend that night, but someone saw you near the gallery."

Graham straightened, his hands clenching at his sides. Lila watched his reaction closely. Graham's piercing blue eyes narrowed behind his glasses. "I don't know what you're talking about, Lila. I already told you where I was that night." His words were clipped, his jaw tightening with each syllable.

Lila held her ground, refusing to be intimidated by his defensive stance. "I understand that, Graham, but I can't ignore this new information. If you were near Evelyn's gallery that night, it could change everything." She took a step closer, her voice softening. "I'm just trying to piece together the truth. You might have seen something that can help Marcus."

"I've already told you, Lila," Graham said, his voice low and controlled, but with an undercurrent of frustration. "I was nowhere near Evelyn's gallery that night. I was in Oakwood Valley, having dinner with an old friend."

"Why would the assistant lie?" Lila countered not wanting to give Ethan's name.

He ran a hand through his salt-and-pepper hair. "I don't know who this assistant is or what they think they saw, but they're mistaken. It wasn't me."

"Well, one of you is lying, and it's probably not him." Lila continued, "I just want the truth."

Graham scoffed, shaking his head. "The truth? It seems like you're more interested in pointing fingers than finding facts." He turned away from her, his attention focused on the paintings he'd been organizing. "I have a show to prepare for, Lila. I don't have time for these baseless accusations."

Lila's mind raced as she watched him dismiss her concerns.

"Graham, please," she implored, reaching out to touch his arm. "If you have nothing to hide, then help me understand. Evelyn was my friend, and I need to her to find out what really happened that night."

"You're obsessed with this, Lila!" he snapped, his voice rising. "You're seeing things that aren't there. Just because I disagreed with Evelyn doesn't mean I killed her!"

Lila flinched slightly at his outburst but held her ground.

Graham ran a hand through his hair, exasperated. "I can't believe you're still harassing me about this. Don't you have anything better to do than interfere with the police investigation? You're not a detective, Lila."

She met his glare unflinchingly. "I'm just trying to figure out the truth, Graham. If you have nothing to hide, why are you so upset? An innocent person would want to help."

The harsh fluorescent lights of the gallery cast an eerie glow on Graham's face as he leaned against the pristine white wall. "You're grasping at straws, Lila," he scoffed, his voice dripping with condescension. "Rumors, that's all you have?"

Lila stood her ground, her blue eyes blazing with determination. "It's more than just rumors, Graham. Julian told me me about your business tactics. How you'd stop at nothing to get what you wanted."

Graham pushed himself off the wall, his tall frame looming over Lila. "Business is business, Lila."

Lila couldn't shake the feeling that there was more to the story. She took a step closer to Graham, her voice low and steady. "Evelyn pulling out of the merger had the potential to ruin you and your gallery."

Graham's eyes narrowed, his voice a low growl. "What exactly are you implying, Lila?"

The tension in the room was palpable, the air thick with unspoken accusations. Lila held Graham's gaze, refusing to back down. "I think you know exactly what

I'm implying, Graham. Evelyn's death was awfully convenient for you, wasn't it?"

Graham's face contorted with rage, his fists clenching at his sides. "How dare you! I had nothing to do with Evelyn's death. I may have disagreed with her about business, but I never would have hurt her."

Lila's instincts screamed at her to push further, to unravel the truth that lingered just beneath the surface. She took a deep breath, her voice calm and measured. "Then help me understand, Graham. Help me clear your name. If you have nothing to hide, you have nothing to fear."

For a moment, Graham seemed to waver, his anger giving way to a flicker of uncertainty. Lila held her breath, wondering if she'd finally reached him, if he'd finally reveal the truth.

But then, as quickly as it had appeared, the moment passed. Graham's face hardened, his eyes cold and distant. "I have nothing more to say to you, Lila. I suggest you leave before I call the police and have you thrown out and arrested for harassment."

Lila's heart sank, realizing that she'd pushed too far. She nodded slowly, backing away from Graham. "This isn't over, Graham. I will find out the truth, with or without your help."

As she turned to leave, Lila could feel Graham's eyes boring into her back, his unspoken threat hanging in the air. She knew she couldn't turn back now. Not when she was so close to figuring out what happened.

She replayed the conversation in her head, searching for clues she might have missed. Graham's insistence that he was out of town, his anger at being questioned, his attempt to shift the focus onto her – it all felt like the actions of a guilty man. But she knew she couldn't prove anything.

Lila pulled out her phone as she walked, her fingers quickly typing out a message to Samantha. "Just left Graham's gallery. He denied being near Evelyn's the night of the murder, but his behavior was suspicious. Definitely hiding something. Heading back to the gallery now to regroup."

She hit send and slipped the phone back into her pocket, her mind already racing with the next steps in her investigation. She needed to talk to Samantha, to bounce ideas off her and get her perspective on the confrontation with Graham. Samantha had always been a sounding board for Lila, her calm demeanor and empathetic nature helping to balance out Lila's impulsive tendencies.

Lila sighed, rubbing her temples as she walked down the street toward her car. Her confrontation with Graham had left her with more questions than answers, but one thing was clear – she couldn't give up. She was going to forget her promise to Marcus.

Chapter 18

Lila stepped into Evelyn's quiet gallery, the chaos of this morning's show set-up over. Sunlight streamed through the high windows, illuminating the paintings that hung silently on the white walls, waiting for their postponed debut. The air felt heavy, somber, yet charged with unspoken anticipation.

She navigated the familiar rooms, her mind still reeling from the tense confrontation with Graham. His sharp words and piercing gaze lingered, unsettling her usually unflappable demeanor. As she approached Evelyn's office, a faint light spilled from the doorway, drawing her like a moth to a flame.

Inside, Samantha sat hunched over Evelyn's desk, surrounded by a sea of legal papers. Her brow furrowed in concentration as she sorted through the documents, a stray lock of hair falling across her face.

"Hey," Lila said softly, not wanting to startle her.

Samantha looked up, her eyes widening in surprise. "Lila, I didn't hear you come in." She tucked the errant hair behind her ear, a small smile tugging at her lips despite the weariness etched on her face.

"What's all this?" Lila gestured to the papers strewn across the desk as she crossed the room to stand beside her friend.

"I was trying to organize some things and accidentally bumped into the filing cabinet." Samantha sighed, running a hand through her hair. "Most of it is just basic legal documents related to the business. Insurance papers, contracts with artists, that sort of thing." She paused, her fingers tracing the edge of a manila envelope. "But I did find this."

Lila leaned in closer, her curiosity piqued. The envelope was unmarked except for a return address stamped in the corner - the name of a law firm she didn't recognize.

"It's from a different lawyer," Samantha explained, her voice hushed as if sharing a secret. "Not Evelyn's usual one."

Lila's heart quickened. "You didn't open it?"

Samantha shook her head, her eyes wide. "I didn't feel right about it. It seemed... personal."

Lila took the envelope, her curiosity piqued. As she unsealed the flap, a small stack of documents slid out, topped by a cover letter.

As she read the first lines, her breath caught in her throat:

Dear Ms. Grey,

I hope this letter finds you well. As per our recent conversation, I am writing to confirm that our firm would be happy to represent you in your cooperation with the ongoing FBI Art Crimes investigation. We understand the delicate nature of this situation and the potential implications for your gallery and personal reputation.

Rest assured, we have extensive experience in dealing with such matters and will work tirelessly to protect your interests throughout this process. Our team is well-versed in the intricacies of art law and has successfully navigated similar cases involving allegations of forgery and fraud within the art world.

We appreciate the trust you've placed in our firm by sharing the details of your involvement and the pressure you've been under. Your decision to come forward with information about the forgery ring operating within the high-end art market is commendable, and we will do everything in our power to ensure your reputation remains intact.

Her heart quickened as she scanned the rest of the documents, the seriousness of the situation sinking in with each page. Evelyn had been preparing for a potential legal battle, that much was clear. Lila's gaze fell on the notes jotted in the margins, the hurried penmanship reflecting Evelyn's anxiety and determination.

Lila continued to search through the stack of documents, her hands trembling slightly as she did so. The words "art forgery" leapt out at her from the pages, and she felt her breath catch in her throat.

"Evelyn was gathering evidence," she said, her voice tinged with disbelief. "She was working with the FBI on exposing a criminal case related to art forgery."

Samantha leaned in closer, her brow furrowed.

Lila's mind raced, trying to piece together the implications. "This is bigger than just gallery disputes or business mergers. Evelyn was onto something huge."

Samantha nodded, her expression grim. "And whoever she suspected must have had a lot to lose. Enough to..." She trailed off, unable to voice the terrible thought.

A heavy silence settled over the room as they absorbed the weight of their discovery. Lila's thoughts turned to Graham, the rival gallery owner she had confronted earlier. But as she scanned the documents again, she realized that his name was conspicuously absent.

"Graham's not mentioned anywhere in here," she said, a hint of doubt creeping into her voice. "Is it possible we have this all wrong?"

Samantha looked up, her eyes wide. "This certainly points to someone other than Graham. It could be someone related to this art forgery case."

"When I confronted Graham earlier, he was adamant that he wasn't anywhere near Evelyn's gallery the night she died. He insists he was out of town, just like he told us before."

Samantha leaned back in Evelyn's chair, her brow furrowed. "But what about Ethan? He was so sure he saw Graham that night."

Lila shook her head, running a hand through her hair. "Graham claims he has no idea who Ethan could have seen. He seemed genuinely confused when I mentioned it, Sam. And now, with these document s..." She gestured to the papers spread across the desk. "I'm starting to wonder if we've been looking in the wrong direction all along."

Lila sat down across the desk from Samantha, her mind still reeling from the discovery of Evelyn's hidden documents. She looked at her friend, seeing the same concern and determination reflected in Samantha's eyes.

"There's something else," Lila said, her voice low. "I overheard Maxine on the phone at the coffee shop earlier. She was talking to someone, and she sounded nervous."

Samantha leaned forward, her brow furrowed. "Nervous? What was she saying?"

"She mentioned 'the feds' like she was worried about getting caught." Lila paused, her gaze drifting to the documents scattered across the desk. "And now, with these papers…"

Samantha nodded, the pieces starting to fall into place. "You think Maxine could be involved in this? In the forgery ring Evelyn was trying to expose?"

Lila stood up, pacing the small office as her mind raced. She had just begun trusting Maxine, seeing a kindred spirit beneath the rebellious exterior. But now, with the overheard conversation at the coffee shop and Evelyn's hidden documents, Lila didn't know what to think.

"I don't know," Lila admitted, running a hand through her hair. "But it's too much of a coincidence, don't you think? Maxine's suspicious phone call, and now these documents…"

Samantha leaned back in her chair, her expression thoughtful. "I never liked Maxine. I didn't trust her, but I never thought she could be capable of something like this. But if she was part of a forgery ring, it would explain why she was so eager to move the focus of the investigation to Graham."

The weight of their suspicions hung heavy in the air, the implications of Maxine's potential involvement sending a chill down Lila's spine. She thought back to the last time she had seen Evelyn, the older woman's face lined with worry and determination.

"Evelyn must have known," Lila said softly, her voice tinged with sadness. "She could have discovered Maxine's connection to the forgery ring, and that's why she was gathering evidence. She could have been trying to stop her."

"We need to be careful," Lila said, her voice steady despite the fear that gnawed at her insides. "If Maxine really is involved, she may have killed Evelyn. She'll do anything to keep her secrets hidden. We can't let her know what we've found."

Samantha agreed, her eyes flickering to the door as if expecting Maxine to burst in at any moment.

"We can't trust anything Maxine has told us," Lila said, her voice barely above a whisper. "We need to start from scratch, Sam. We need to dig into Evelyn's past ourselves."

Samantha nodded, her eyes wide with a mixture of fear and determination. "But where do we even start? Evelyn was always so private about her life before the gallery."

"We'll start researching tomorrow," Lila said, her voice filled with renewed determination as she stood and looked out into the gallery. She turned to Samantha, who was still seated at the desk, her fingers absently tracing the edges of the incriminating documents. "Sam, I need you to do a deeper dive into the gallery records. Look for anything unusual – large purchases, sudden cancellations, artists who might have been involved in the forgery ring. Even the smallest detail could be important."

Samantha nodded, her eyes bright with purpose. "I'll go through everything. There might be patterns or anomalies we didn't notice before, especially now that we know about the forgery ring."

Lila nodded, her mind already racing with possibilities. "I'll focus on researching art publications and newsletters. There might be clues hidden in old articles or exhibition reviews."

Lila paused, her fingers tracing the edges of the desk. "But what about Graham?" she said, her brow furrowing. "I was so sure he was involved somehow."

Samantha leaned back in Evelyn's chair, considering. "I know you had your suspicions, but think about it. There's nothing in these documents that points to him. And this is definitely a more probable lead."

Lila's mind drifted back to her confrontation with Graham, the way he had bristled at her accusations. She had been so convinced of his guilt, so ready to believe the worst of him. But now, with the evidence of the forgery scandal laid out before them, she found herself second-guessing her earlier beliefs.

"You're right," Lila admitted, a hint of resignation in her voice. "He was defensive, sure, but that doesn't mean he's involved in this forgery case Evelyn was working on."

Samantha nodded, her eyes scanning the documents once more. "If anything, this shifts our focus away from Graham entirely. Evelyn's killer is probably someone tied to this forgery ring, not a rival gallery owner."

"I may owe him an apology," Lila said softly, more to herself than to Samantha. She felt a pang of guilt at the realization. "I let my emotions cloud my judgment."

Samantha reached across the desk, placing a comforted hand on Lila's arm. "Don't be too hard on yourself. We're all just trying to make sense of this."

Lila nodded, drawing strength from her friend's support.

With a deep breath, Lila straightened her shoulders, a newfound determination settling over her. "Okay," she said, her voice steady. "Let's figure out our next move. We have a killer to catch."

Lila and Samantha exchanged a determined look, the weight of their discovery hanging in the air between them. Samantha nodded.

"We have to tell Marcus," Lila said. "These documents... they could change everything."

Samantha nodded again, her brow furrowed with concern. "But what about Maxine? What do we tell her?"

Lila felt a wave of conflicting emotions wash over her. Maxine was starting to become her friend, but the overheard phone conversation at the coffee shop had planted seeds of doubt in her mind. She couldn't shake the feeling that Maxine was somehow involved in the forgery scandal, but she had no concrete proof.

"I don't know," Lila said, her voice heavy with resignation. "But we can't keep this to ourselves. We have to trust that Marcus will handle it with discretion."

Samantha hesitated for a moment before nodding in agreement. "You're right. We have to do what's best for the investigation, even if it means..." She trailed off, unable to finish the thought.

"I'll tell Marcus about what I heard at the coffee shop," Lila said, her voice resigned. "But Sam, you have to promise not to mention my visit to Graham's gallery. I gave him my word that I would stay out of it."

Samantha's eyes widened in surprise, but she quickly nodded in understanding. "Of course, Lila. I won't say a word."

Lila felt a wave of relief wash over her, grateful for her friend's loyalty. She knew that keeping secrets from Marcus was a risk, but she couldn't bring herself to admit to him that she had still involved herself in the investigation after she had said she would stay out of it.

With a deep breath, Lila gathered the documents and stood up from the desk. "Okay," she said, her voice filled with determination. "I'll go see him tomorrow after I do the research on Evelyn's past."

CHAPTER 19

L ila pushed aside her sketchbook and rubbed her tired eyes. She had needed a break form her search, but sketching wasn't helping. The dining table was a sea of papers - interview notes, gallery brochures, suspect lists. Her gaze caught on Maxine's name, underlined in red. She sighed and reached for her coffee mug, taking a long sip of the now lukewarm liquid.

Lila decided to move away from Evelyn's background research and look into Maxine instead.

"What are you hiding, Maxine?" Lila muttered to herself. The doubts nagged at her. She grabbed her computer and with a few decisive keystrokes, she opened a browser window and typed in Maxine's name.

Social media profiles popped up first - artsy Instagram shots, cryptic Twitter posts. Maxine's online presence seemed superficial, all sharp edges and bold statements. Everything seemed to revolve around her art, nothing personal. Lila scrolled through, scanning for any hints or clues that might reveal something deeper.

Next, she dug into newsletter archives. Maxine's professional achievements were well-documented: glowing reviews of her exhibitions, profiles in art magazines. But something felt off, a hole where the full story should have been.

Lila's eyes narrowed as she scrolled through the search results. There was plenty about Maxine's recent work and gallery shows, but very little about her background or early career.

"That can't be right," Lila muttered, her fingers flying over the keyboard as she refined her search. She added terms like "early work" and "background" but came up empty.

Frustrated, Lila leaned back in her chair, her mind racing. Everyone had a past, especially in the art world where connections and education often played a crucial role in an artist's career.

On a hunch, Lila opened a new tab and searched for art forgery cases from the past decade. She skimmed through news articles and legal reports, her heart pounding as she looked for any connection to Maxine or Evelyn.

Suddenly, a name caught her eye. In a small article about a forgery ring busted five years ago, there was a mention of an " unnamed promising young artist" who had been implicated but never charged.

Lila's thoughts drifted to when Lila last saw Maxine, and the parts of the phone conversation she had overheard

Lila scrolled further, searching for any clues that might shed light on what she had found so far. She landed on an old news article from an obscure art blog. The headline caught her eye: "Rising Star Accused in Forgery Scandal." Lila's heart raced as she clicked the link, a sense of dark foreboding washing over her.

As Lila scrolled through the article, snippets of information painted a picture of a once-close relationship between Maxine and Evelyn that had turned sour. Mentions of heated arguments at gallery openings, passive-aggressive comments in interviews.

A name caught her eye: Henry Marsh, a prominent art dealer who had worked closely with Evelyn in the past. Lila scribbled down his contact details, a flicker of hope igniting in her chest. He was the only one who could possibly explain the rift between the two women.

She reached for her phone, pulse quickening as she dialed the number. The line clicked, and a gruff voice answered. "Henry Marsh speaking."

"Mr. Marsh, my name is Lila Montgomery. I'm looking into the death of Evelyn Grey, and I was hoping you could provide some insight into her relationship with Maxine Banks."

There was a weighty pause. "Ah, yes. Evelyn and Maxine. Quite the tangled web, that one."

Lila leaned forward, hanging onto his every word. "What can you tell me about their falling out?"

Henry sighed, the sound heavy with the weight of years. "It was a scandal, plain and simple. Maxine allegedly forged Evelyn's signature to process a sale for a piece Evelyn never would have sold. It nearly cost Evelyn her reputation."

Lila's breath caught in her throat. Maxine forged a signature. That seemed a far cry from art forgery. The implications swirled in her mind, dark and unsettling. "What happened to the piece?"

"Disappeared," Henry said. "Along with any hard evidence linking Maxine to the crime. But Evelyn knew. And she never forgave her."

Lila scribbled furiously in her notebook, the pieces of the puzzle shifting into a new, disturbing configuration. "Thank you, Mr. Marsh. You've been a great help."

As she hung up, Lila sat back in her chair, feeling slightly guilty because Henry obviously thought Lila was with the police.

Lila stared at the notes before her, the weight of the revelation settling heavily on her shoulders. Maxine's past was more complicated than she had ever imagined. The signature forgery accusation could have lead to more. And that cast a dark shadow over their current investigation. Lila couldn't shake the feeling that it was all connected somehow.

Lila continued her deep dive into the online archives, determined to uncover more about the forgery scandal that had rocked Evelyn and Maxine's relationship. She clicked through page after page of search results, her eyes scanning for any mention of the incident to back up what Henry had told her.

Finally, she stumbled upon a digital archive of an old art magazine, its pages slightly yellowed and crackling with age even on the screen. Lila's heart raced as she scrolled through the issues. She paused on an issue from five years ago.

And there it was. A feature article from nearly a decade ago, the headline bold and accusing: "The Dark Side of the Art World"

Lila's eyes narrowed as she scanned the issue of the obscure art magazine, fingers tracing the faded text. There was a small blurb that confirmed Henry's story. Evelyn had indeed accused a trusted associate of forgery years ago, though no names were mentioned.

The timing and context aligned perfectly with Maxine's situation.

If Maxine was truly involved, as Henry suggested, it painted a disturbing picture of her character. To forge Evelyn's signature, to betray her trust so blatantly...it spoke of a ruthless ambition, a willingness to cross lines that should never be crossed.

Lila leaned back in her chair, the weight of the revelation settling heavily on her shoulders. The Maxine she thought she knew, the grieving friend and colleague, now seemed like a stranger. A suspect.

A chill ran down her spine as she considered the implications. If Maxine had been willing to commit forgery, to jeopardize Evelyn's reputation...what else was she capable of?

Lila's gaze drifted to the threatening photographs on her desk. The thought made her stomach churn.

She shook her head. She needed proof, concrete evidence before she could confront Maxine. With a heavy sigh, she gathered her notes, tucking them carefully into her bag.

Lila's mind raced as she stood up from the table, her chair scraping against the hardwood floor. She paced the length of her apartment, her mind churning with the weight of her discoveries. The old floorboards creaked beneath her feet, a rhythmic accompaniment to her troubled thoughts.

Memories of Maxine flooded her mind, snapshots of their past interactions. But now, with the revelation of the forgery scandal, Lila found herself questioning everything.

She closed her eyes, recalling a moment from Evelyn's memorial service. Maxine had approached her, offering condolences and a shoulder to lean on. "If there's anything I can do, anything at all, just say the word," she had murmured, her hand resting on Lila's arm. At the time, Lila had been touched by the gesture, grateful for the support.

Lila shook her head, trying to clear the doubts that clouded her judgment. She shouldn't confront Maxine about this, not yet. But, she needed more information, more evidence to back up her growing suspicions. Maxine would likely shift suspicion to someone else, probably Graham.

With a sigh, she turned from the window and reached for her phone. Her fingers hovered over the keypad, hesitating for a moment before dialing a familiar number.

"Hey, Maxine," she said, injecting a note of casual warmth into her voice. "I was wondering if you might have time to grab a coffee later this week? I've been going through some of Evelyn's old papers, and I thought you might be able to help me make sense of a few things."

She held her breath, waiting for Maxine's response. If she could keep her close, keep the lines of communication open, maybe Maxine would let something slip, reveal a clue that could crack the case wide open.

"Of course," Maxine replied, her tone smooth and unruffled. "I'm always happy to help, Lila. Just name the time and place."

Lila felt a flicker of unease at the easy agreement, but she pushed it aside. "Great. How about tomorrow afternoon at the coffee shop? Say, around 2?"

"I'll be there."

As Lila ended the call and set her phone down on the table, the weight of her suspicions lay heavy in her heart.

Lila stood, pacing the length of her apartment as her mind raced. If Evelyn had been planning to come forward with more evidence about the forgery scandal, to expose Maxine's alleged misdeeds to the world, it would have been a catastrophic blow to Maxine's career. The art world was an unforgiving place, and a revelation like that could have ruined her.

"Motive," Lila whispered, her heart sinking. "She had motive."

But even as the pieces seemed to fall into place, Lila couldn't shake the nagging doubts that plagued her. Maxine had been so convincing in her grief, so seemingly genuine in her desire to help. Could it all have been an act?

Lila shook her head, her resolve hardening. She couldn't let her emotions cloud her judgment, couldn't let her personal feelings for Maxine blind her to the evidence before her. She had to approach this with a clear head and an unwavering commitment to the truth.

Chapter 20

The delicate chime of the bell over the door signaled Lila's arrival at the quaint coffee shop nestled on Willow Creek's main street. She inhaled the rich aroma of freshly brewed coffee as she approached the counter, her mind already swirling with thoughts of the impending conversation with Maxine.

"The usual, Lila?" the barista asked with a friendly smile.

"Yes, thanks," Lila replied absentmindedly, her eyes darting to the window as she waited. She couldn't shake the unease that had settled in her stomach like a lead weight.

Moments later, coffee in hand, Lila settled into a seat by the window. She stirred the steaming liquid, watching the swirls of cream dissolve. Outside, the hustle and bustle of the town carried on, oblivious to the turmoil raging inside her.

The bell chimed again, snapping Lila from her reverie. Maxine strode in, her vibrant hair and edgy style commanding attention as always. Lila plastered on a smile as Maxine approached, noting the subtle tension in her friend's shoulders beneath her leather jacket.

"Lila!" Maxine greeted warmly, leaning in for a quick embrace. "How are you?"

"Maxine, so good to see you," Lila returned, gesturing for her to sit. "I hear your New York show is coming up soon. That's exciting!"

Maxine's eyes lit up as she launched into details about the upcoming show. Lila nodded along, sipping her coffee, but her mind kept drifting to the real reason for their meeting: to judge Maxine's reaction to Graham.

"...and the curator is thrilled with the new pieces," Maxine was said, her hands animated. "It's going to be a fantastic show."

"I'm so happy for you, Maxine. You've worked hard for this," Lila said, pushing down her own turbulent thoughts. She couldn't let on to what she knew about Maxine's history.

"Thanks, Lila. That means a lot coming from you." Maxine's smile faltered slightly, her gaze searching Lila's face.

The weight of unspoken words hung heavy between them. Lila took another sip of coffee, steeling herself for the conversation ahead. She had to tread carefully, to untangle the web of secrets without getting caught in the threads herself.

Lila set her cup down, the soft clink of ceramic on the table serving as a subtle shift in the conversation. "I actually wanted to talk to you about something else," she began, her voice measured. "I had a run-in with Graham the other day."

Maxine's eyebrows shot up, her interest piqued. "Oh? What happened?"

"I confronted him about Ethan seeing him near the gallery the night Evelyn was murdered. Graham had claimed before that he had been out of town, but apparently that wasn't the case." Lila watched Maxine's reaction carefully, noting the flicker of success in her eyes.

"Really? That's interesting." Maxine leaned forward, her elbows resting on the table. "What did he say?"

"He got defensive, accused me of being 'obsessed' with the investigation." Lila shrugged, feigning nonchalance. "But it just doesn't add up. Why would he lie about his whereabouts?"

Maxine seized the opportunity, her words tumbling out in a rush. "Lila, I've been thinking the same thing. Graham is the only one with a real motive here. He had financial troubles, a history of aggressive business tactics. And we all know how strained his relationship with Evelyn was."

Lila nodded, encouraging Maxine to continue. She needed to hear this, to see how far Maxine would go to paint Graham as the villain.

"That merger between their galleries? It was a humiliating concession for Graham. He resented Evelyn for being the stronger businessperson, for always coming out on top." Maxine's eyes flashed with conviction. "And he has no confirmed alibi for the night of the murder. His behavior since then has been erratic at best. It all points to him, Lila."

Lila listened, absorbing every word, every inflection. Maxine was certainly convincing, but Lila couldn't shake the nagging feeling that something wasn't quite right. She thought back to the information she'd uncovered about Maxine's past, the accusations of forgery, the bitter falling out with Evelyn.

"You might be right," Lila said slowly, keeping her true thoughts hidden behind a mask of agreement. "Graham does seem like the most logical suspect. I just want to be sure we're not missing anything."

Maxine reached across the table, patting Lila's hand reassuringly. "Trust me, Lila. Graham is our guy. The sooner we can prove it, the sooner we can put this thing behind us."

Lila forced a smile, her skin crawling at Maxine's touch. But she couldn't let her suspicions show, not now. She had to play along, to keep Maxine thinking she was on her side.

"You're probably right," Lila conceded, her voice soft. "I just hate to think that someone we know could be capable of something so awful."

Maxine nodded, a flicker of something unreadable in her eyes. "I know, Lila. It's hard to accept. But sometimes, people surprise us in the worst ways possible."

Maxine glanced at her watch, her brow furrowing slightly. "I hate to cut this short, but I really should get back to the studio. I have a painting to finish for my upcoming show in New York." She stood up, smoothing her hand over hair.

"Of course," Lila said, rising to her feet as well. "I don't want to keep you from your work."

Maxine flashed her a warm smile, the same one that had once made Lila feel welcomed and understood. Now, it felt like a carefully crafted mask.

"We'll talk soon, Lila. Keep me posted on any new developments, okay?"

Lila nodded, returned Maxine's smile with one of her own. "Will do. Good luck with your painting."

She watched as Maxine strode out of the coffee shop, her confident gait and self-assured presence drawing the eyes of the other patrons. It was only when Maxine had disappeared from view that Lila allowed her own smile to fade, replaced by a heavy sigh.

Sinking back into her chair, Lila buried her face in her hands, feeling the weight of the investigation pressing down on her like a physical burden. Every new piece of information, every contradictory statement, seemed to pull her further into a labyrinth of secrets and lies.

Lila knew she needed more proof before going to Marcus. She couldn't risk tipping her hand too soon, not when Maxine was so skilled at deflection and manipulation. She gathered her things and stepped out into the bustling street.

The parking lot was nearly empty when Lila emerged from the coffee shop, the sun glinting off the tops of the few cars scattered about.

As she approached the driver's side door, a flicker of white caught her eye. Lila frowned, noticing a small piece of paper tucked beneath her windshield wiper. Curious, she plucked it free and unfolded it.

Her heart skipped a beat as she read the message scrawled in neat, blocky letters: "Stop digging or you'll regret it."

Lila's breath caught in her throat, a chill racing down her spine despite the warm afternoon sun. She whirled around, her eyes scanning the parking lot for any sign of who might have left the note. But the space was deserted.

This was different from the photographs. Those had been unsettling, yes, but there had been a degree of ambiguity to them. They could have been explained away as coincidence or maybe even a misguided attempt at art. But this note... there was no mistaking its intent.

"Stop digging or you'll regret it." The words seemed to pulse on the page, each letter a stark reminder of the danger she faced. This wasn't a vague warning or a subtle hint. It was a direct threat, a clear message that someone was watching her, tracking her movements, and was willing to take action if she didn't back off.

She felt her hands tighten around the slip of paper, knowing that whoever wrote this wanted to scare her away from uncovering the truth.

But after the initial fear, Lila felt a surge of determination. This threat was proof that her investigation was on the right track, that she was asking the right questions.

Lila snapped a quick photo of the message, ensuring she had a digital copy for safekeeping. Then she folded the original and tucked it into her bag as she slid into the driver's seat.

As she turned the key in the ignition, Lila's mind was already racing ahead, plotting her next move. She knew she'd have to be more careful now.

As Lila navigated the familiar streets of Willow Creek, her thoughts drifted to her recent conversations with Marcus. The detective's words echoed in her mind, his warnings about the dangers of her involvement growing louder with each passing block.

"You're not trained for this, Lila," he had cautioned her, his blue eyes filled with concern. "Let the police do their job. Don't do anything reckless. You could become the killer's next target"

She had eventually heeded his advice and stepped back from the investigation. But the questions had never truly left her. They lingered in the back of her mind, whispering doubts and theories. And then, with one sentence from Ethan, Lila had found herself drawn back into the investigation.

As she gripped the steering wheel, she realized why Marcus had been warning her all along. But she had ignored his words, too focused on playing detective and too confident to see the potential dangers.

Lila's mind flashed back to the day she and Sam had found Evelyn. The images of Evelyn's lifeless body forever seared into her memory - this was no simple crime of passion. Whoever had killed Evelyn was dangerous, ruthless, and clearly willing to do whatever it took to protect their secrets.

A shiver ran down Lila's spine as she realized, *They're watching me now. They must know I'm getting closer.*

As much as it pained her to admit it, Marcus was right. Lila knew she couldn't continue on as she had been- rushing headlong into danger, chasing down leads without regard for her own safety - that was a surefire way to end up like Evelyn.

CHAPTER 21

Lila stood before the Willow Creek Police Station, the sudden chill wind tugging at her skirt. She took a deep breath, steadying herself. Marcus wouldn't be pleased to see her, not after his warnings to stay away from the investigation.

She pushed through the heavy doors. Approaching the front desk, Lila mustered her most confident tone. "I need to speak with Detective Reed. It's urgent."

The officer glanced up from his paperwork. "He's wrapping up another case. Take a seat and he'll be with you shortly."

Lila nodded, retreating to a worn leather chair in the lobby. As she waited, her mind raced with the revelations of the past few days. The threatening note left on her windshield. Her growing suspicions about Maxine.

The click of a door jolted her back to the present. Lila straightened, steeling herself for the confrontation to come. Marcus emerged from the depths of the station, his expression a mix of weariness and resignation. She stood to meet him, determined to make him understand the weight of her discoveries.

Marcus approached with a heavy step, his gaze locking onto Lila. He gestured towards his office, a silent invitation tinged with reluctance. Lila followed. As they entered the cramped space, Marcus shut the door with a soft click, sealing them off from the bustling station.

He sank into his chair, the leather creaking beneath him. "Alright, Lila. What have you got for me this time?"

Lila leaned forward, her words tumbling out with urgency. "I overheard Maxine on the phone at the coffee shop. She was talking about being caught by the feds, Marcus. The feds."

Marcus's brow furrowed, his interest piqued despite his reservations. "Go on."

"So, I did some digging. Looked into Evelyn's past shows and contacts, trying to find anything that might fit." Lila paused, gathering her thoughts. "And then I met with Maxine. Tried to feel her out, see if she'd let anything slip."

"I take it that didn't go well?"

Lila shook her head, a mirthless smile playing at her lips. "No. But when I got back to my car, I found this." She pulled out the note, the menacing words seared into her memory. "This is more than just the photographs, Marcus. Someone doesn't want me asking questions."

Marcus took the note, his eyes scanning the text. Again, Lila saw a flicker of concern crack his stoic façade. He looked up at her, his voice low and urgent. "Lila, this is serious. You need to be careful. I thought you were going to stop your investigation."

"I know, and I was. But I'm so close." Lila's gaze was unwavering, though remorseful, her determination etched into every line of her face. "Whoever's behind this, they're scared. They wouldn't have threatened me if I wasn't onto something."

Marcus leaned forward, his elbows resting on the desk, his hands clasped tightly together. "Lila, I need you to listen to me. You're not a detective. This isn't your job." His tone was firm, but tinged with an undercurrent of worry. "Every time you come in here with new information, you're putting yourself and this investigation at risk. You were threatened."

Lila bristled, her own frustration rising to meet his. "I know I'm not a cop, Marcus. But I'm not just going to sit back and do nothing."

"I understand that, but—"

"No, I don't think you do." Lila urged. "I'm close, Marcus. I can feel it. Whoever's behind this, they're getting nervous. They wouldn't have threatened me otherwise."

Marcus ran a hand over his face, the late nights and endless leads etched into the lines around his eyes. "That's exactly my point, Lila. They threatened you. This isn't a game. If you keep pushing, if you keep sticking your nose where it doesn't belong, you could find yourself in real danger."

Lila met his gaze, her jaw set. "I can't back down. Not now. If I stop, they win." Her voice softened, a pleading note creeping in. "I need you to trust me, Marcus. I need you to let me see this through."

Marcus stood, his tall frame unfolding as he walked around the desk. He placed his hands on Lila's shoulders, his grip firm, his eyes locked on hers. "I do trust you, Lila. But I also have a duty to protect you." He trailed off, the unspoken fears hanging heavy in the air between them.

Lila felt the weight of his words, the genuine concern that underscored his frustration. She knew he was right. She was taking risks, putting herself in the line of fire.

She stepped back, Marcus's hands falling away. "I'll be careful. I promise. But I have to see this through. For Evelyn. For myself." Her voice was steady, the determination in her eyes unwavering.

Lila took a deep breath, steeling herself for what she was about to reveal. She reached into her bag and pulled out a manila folder, the edges slightly worn from her constant reviewing of its contents.

"There's more, Marcus." She reached into her bag, pulling out a manila folder. "Samantha and I found these documents in Evelyn's office. They were mixed in with other legal papers. We weren't sure what to make of them at first, but now..." She trailed off, her fingers tracing the edge of the folder.

Marcus's eyebrows raised, his curiosity piqued despite his reservations. "What are you talking about, Lila?"

"These are legal documents we found hidden in Evelyn's office," Lila explained. "They show that Evelyn was working with the FBI, Marcus. She was helping them investigate an art forgery ring."

Marcus's eyes widened as he flipped open the folder, scanning the contents. Lila watched as his expression shifted from skepticism to shock, then to understanding.

Marcus's face grew serious as he scanned the documents, his brow furrowing deeper with each page he turned.

Lila leaned forward, her heart racing. "Do you see now why I couldn't just let this go? Evelyn was onto something big, Marcus. Something that got her killed."

Marcus leaned back in his chair, rubbing his temples. "Alright, Lila. You've made your point. But this doesn't change the fact that you're in danger. Whoever's behind this clearly knows you're investigating, and they're not afraid to make threats."

Lila stood, gathering her things. She could feel the weight of Marcus's concern, but also the grudging acceptance that she was too deeply involved to back out now. "I understand the risks, Marcus. I'll be careful, I promise."

As Lila left Marcus's office, she felt a chill run down her spine. She paused at the front desk and looked back toward Marcus's office. The receptionist, now a young woman with kind eyes, looked up at her. "Everything alright, Miss Montgomery?"

Lila forced a smile, the action feeling foreign on her face. "Yes, thank you. Just lost in thought."

As she stepped out into the gloomy afternoon, the weight of Marcus's warning settled heavily on her shoulders. A light rain had started, echoing the tumultuous thoughts in her head.

She pulled her jacket tighter around her, a futile attempt at shielding herself from the rain as she walked to her car.

Inside the car, Lila sat for a moment, her hands gripping the steering wheel, her eyes staring unseeing at the rain-streaked windshield. Marcus's words echoed in her head, a constant reminder of the risks she was taking.

CHAPTER 22

Lila stepped inside the gallery, her footsteps echoing in the empty space. She scanned the walls, taking in the vivid splashes of color, but her mind was elsewhere. The threatening note she had received earlier that day weighed heavily in her thoughts.

Lila made her way towards the back office, her unease growing with each step. She had only returned to retrieve the invitations she had forgotten, but the eerily quiet gallery set her nerves on edge. As she approached Evelyn's office, a faint rustling sound caught her attention. The door stood slightly ajar.

Cautiously, Lila peered through the gap. Her eyes widened at the sight of Maxine rifling through Evelyn's desk drawers, papers strewn haphazardly across the surface. Maxine's movements were hurried and agitated, her brows furrowed in concentration as she searched for something.

Lila stood frozen in the doorway, shock coursing through her veins.

Maxine muttered under her breath as she searched, her words too low for Lila to make out. The artist's face was a mask of desperation, her usual cool demeanor replaced by raw, unbridled panic. Sweat beaded on her forehead, and her chest heaved with rapid, shallow breaths.

"Maxine?"

Maxine's head snapped up, her eyes wide with panic. She stumbled back from the desk, papers fluttering to the floor. "Lila! I... I can explain."

Lila's heart pounded in her chest as she stepped fully into the office, her eyes never leaving Maxine's panicked face. The air felt thick with tension, the silence broken only by the soft flutter of papers settling on the hardwood floor.

"How did you get in here, Maxine?" Lila asked, shocked. She glanced around the room, taking in the chaos of scattered documents and upended drawers. The usually immaculate office had been ransacked, with Evelyn's personal effects strewn about haphazardly.

Maxine swallowed hard, her hands trembling as she smoothed down her shirt. "Sam," she said quickly, her eyes darting to the door behind Lila. "She let me in. I told her I needed to pick up some paperwork for my upcoming show."

Lila's brow furrowed, disbelief etching across her features. She knew Samantha would never allow Maxine unsupervised access to Evelyn's private office. And why would there be any paperwork for a show that wasn't being held here. The lie hung heavy in the air between them.

Lila crossed her arms, her gaze unwavering. "Why are you rifling through Evelyn's desk. If Sam knew you were coming, what you needed would have been on top."

Maxine took a deep breath, her hands trembling slightly. "I've been trying to help find out who killed Evelyn. I thought... I thought there might be clues here, something to support your investigation."

Lila raised an eyebrow, her suspicion growing. Maxine's flustered demeanor and erratic behavior told a different story. Lila knew Maxine wasn't telling her everything.

"Sam works here, we have already done that. We told you that." Lila stepped closer, her eyes locked on Maxine's. "What are you really looking for, Maxine?"

Maxine's gaze darted around the room, avoiding Lila's intense stare. She fidgeted with the hem of her jacket, her words tumbling out in a rush. "Maybe you missed something. I... I just wanted to help. Evelyn meant so much to me, to all of us. I couldn't just sit by and do nothing."

Lila's mind raced, piecing together the clues. She recalled the suspicious phone conversation she had overheard at the café, Maxine's hushed words about the feds. The strange behavior, the evasive answers.

Maxine was lying.

Lila's suspicions reached a tipping point. She couldn't ignore the evidence any longer.

She took a deep breath, steeling herself for the confrontation that was about to unfold. With a steady gaze, Lila spoke, her voice low but firm. "Maxine, I think it's time we had an honest conversation."

Maxine's eyes widened, a flicker of panic crossing her features. "What do you mean, Lila? I've been nothing but honest with you."

Lila shook her head, her patience wearing thin. "No, you haven't. I overheard your phone call at the café, talking about the feds. And then there's the allegedly forged signature and the legal documents I found in Evelyn's office about a forgery ring."

She took a step closer, her eyes never leaving Maxine's. "Your behavior has been erratic and suspicious. It all points to your involvement in something deeper, something you're not telling me."

Maxine's hands trembled slightly as she gripped the edge of the desk, her knuckles turning white. "I don't know what you're talking about, Lila. You're seeing things that aren't there."

Lila's frustration mounted, her voice rising with each word. "Stop lying to me, Maxine! I know you're hiding something." She gestured around the office, her eyes fiery with determination. "You're not just here to help. You're looking for something specific, something that could implicate you. Tell me the truth, Maxine. What really happened between you and Evelyn?"

Maxine's façade crumbled, her shoulders sagging under the weight of Lila's accusation. She averted her gaze, her voice barely above a whisper. "You don't understand, Lila. It's complicated..."

Lila folded her arms, her stance unyielding. "Then help me understand. I won't stop until I uncover the truth, no matter where it leads."

The tension in the room was palpable. Lila's heart raced as she waited for Maxine's response, knowing that the next words out of her mouth could change everything.

"The truth, Maxine. It's time to come clean. No more lies, no more games. We both deserve answers, and I won't rest until I have them."

Maxine's eyes darted around the room, her fingers fidgeting with the hem of her shirt. "I don't know what you're talking about, Lila. I would never do anything to hurt Evelyn or the gallery."

Lila crossed her arms, her gaze unwavering. "Really?"

"You're being ridiculous." Maxine's voice wavered slightly. She turned away from Lila, busying herself with straightening a stack of papers on the desk. "I'm just trying to help figure out what happened to Evelyn, that's all."

Lila wasn't buying it. She could see the tension in Maxine's shoulders, the way her hands trembled ever so slightly.

"What about the forgery rumors, Maxine? And the legal documents I found in Evelyn's office?" Lila pressed on, taking a step closer. "Your behavior has been erratic lately. It all adds up to something you're not telling me."

Maxine's façade began to crack. She ran a hand through her short, vibrant hair, her breath coming in short, sharp bursts. Lila could see the internal struggle playing out across Maxine's face.

Maxine's shoulders slumped, the fight seeming to drain out of her. She turned to face Lila, her eyes glistening with unshed tears. "You're right," she whispered, her voice barely audible. "There's so much I haven't told you."

Lila held her breath, waiting for Maxine to continued. The air in the office felt thick, charged with the weight of long-held secrets finally coming to light.

Maxine sank into Evelyn's chair, her fingers tracing the worn leather armrests. "It's true that I was involved in forgeries years ago," she began, her gaze fixed on a point beyond Lila. "I was young, desperate to make a name for myself in the art world. I made terrible choices, ones that nearly cost me everything."

Lila held her breath, waiting for Maxine to continue. The air in the office felt heavy.

"But I got out." Maxine took a shaky breath, her gaze fixed on a point just over Lila's shoulder. "Evelyn helped me. We were working together. To bring down the forgery ring."

Lila's eyes widened in surprise. Of all the scenarios she had imagined, this wasn't one of them. "What?" she breathed, her mind reeling. Lila studied Maxine's face, searching for any hint of deception. The confession about the forgery was a breakthrough, but something still didn't sit right.

Lila's instincts told her there was more to the story. She couldn't shake the feeling that Maxine was still holding something back.

"Maxine," Lila began, "I need to know something, and I need you to be completely honest with me." She paused, gathering her courage.

Lila's heart pounded in her chest as she forced out the words that had been haunting her. "Did you kill Evelyn?"

Maxine's eyes widened in shock, her face draining of color. She stumbled back as if physically struck by Lila's words, her hip bumping against the edge of Evelyn's desk. Papers scattered to the floor, the soft whisper of falling documents the only sound in the sudden, deafening silence.

"Kill Evelyn?" Maxine's voice was barely above a whisper, thick with disbelief and anguish. "How could you even think that?"

Tears welled up in Maxine's eyes, spilling over and trailing down her cheeks. Her hands trembled as she gripped the edge of the desk for support, her knuckles turning white with the force of her grip.

"Evelyn was my mentor, my friend," Maxine continued, her voice gaining strength even as it cracked with emotion.

"What about the phone call I overheard at the café?" Lila asked, her tone gentle but firm. "And why were you searching through Evelyn's desk just now?"

Maxine's gaze darted around the room, avoiding Lila's questioned stare. She fidgeted with her hands, twisting a silver ring on her finger. "I... I was just looking for something. Something personal."

Lila raised an eyebrow. "In Evelyn's desk? After her death?"

"It's not what you think," Maxine said quickly, but her voice lacked conviction.

The more Maxine tried to explain, the more Lila's suspicions grew. The pieces were there, but they didn't quite fit together. Not yet.

"Maxine, I want to believe you, but you're not giving me the whole truth." Lila's words hung in the air, a challenge and a plea all at once.

Maxine's shoulders sagged, and she sank back into the chair, her head in her hands. The silence stretched between them, heavy with unspoken secrets.

With a sigh, Lila approached the desk, her arms crossed. She studied Maxine's hunched form, searching for any flicker of truth in her body language. "Maxine, I can't help you if you don't talk to me. What really happened between you and Evelyn?"

Maxine looked up, her eyes rimmed with red. "I... I can't tell you everything. Not yet. But I swear, I didn't kill her."

Lila's frustration mounted, but she tried to keep her voice steady. "Then give me something, anything, to prove your innocence. Because right now, all the evidence points to you."

"I know how it looks." Maxine's voice was barely a whisper. "But there's more to the story, Lila. Things I can't explain, not without putting others at risk."

"I want to believe you, Maxine. I really do. But I need more than just your word." Lila turned to face her, her eyes pleaded. "Help me understand."

Maxine's gaze met Lila's, and for a moment, she saw a flicker of vulnerability. But just as quickly, it was gone, replaced by a steely resolve.

"I'm sorry, Lila. I can't tell you more. Not now."

Lila's phone vibrated in her pocket, breaking the tense silence. She hesitated, her eyes still locked on Maxine, but the insistent buzzing couldn't be ignored. With a frustrated sigh, she pulled out her phone and glanced at the screen.

It was a text from Sam. "Urgent. New information about Graham."

Lila's heart raced as she read the message, her mind already spinning with possibilities. Sam must have uncovered something significant, something that couldn't wait. She looked back at Maxine, who sat motionless in Evelyn's chair, her gaze distant and troubled.

"I have to go," Lila said abruptly, shoving her phone back into her pocket. "But this conversation isn't over, Maxine. I will get to the bottom of this."

Without waiting for a response, Lila turned on her heel and strode out of the office, her mind reeling with unanswered questions.

Chapter 23

Lila stepped out of the gallery, the door slamming shut behind her with an ominous thud. The confrontation with Maxine still echoed in her mind, a chorus of accusations and deflections that left her head spinning. She paused on the stone steps, drawing in a deep breath of the crisp evening air, trying to steady herself.

Maxine's behavior had been strange. Lila replayed their interactions in her mind, searching for some concrete evidence, something she had said, but it remained maddeningly out of reach.

With leaden steps, Lila made her way toward her car, parked in the shadowy alcove beside the gallery. The night seemed to press in around her, the air thick with unspoken secrets and unresolved tensions. Every rustle of leaves, every distant car horn, set her nerves on edge.

Maxine's words echoed in her head, each syllable a puzzle piece that refused to fit. "We were working together. To bring down the forgery ring." The claim hung in the air, tantalizing yet elusive, like smoke dissipating in the breeze.

Could it be true? Had Maxine been working with the FBI too? The idea seemed far-fetched for Evelyn to work so closely with someone that Lila had never met before.

She thought back to the legal documents she had found in Evelyn's office, the ones that hinted at a deeper involvement with law enforcement. At the time, she had assumed they pertained only to Evelyn, but now... could Maxine have been mentioned as well.

As she neared the corner, the sound of low voices caught her attention. Lila froze, her heartbeat quickening. She recognized one of the voices immediately - it was Marcus, deep in conversation with another officer. Their words were muffled, indistinct, but the urgency in their tones was unmistakable.

Lila pressed herself against the rough brick wall, straining to catch snippets of their conversation without being seen. Lila closed her eyes, fighting back a wave of frustration. She knew she couldn't confront them directly, not without tipping her hand and risking Marcus shutting her out of the investigation entirely.

Lila edged closer to the corner, her steps slow, careful not to make a sound. The rough texture of the brick wall scraped against her palm as she steadied herself, inching forward until the voices became clearer.

"Ethan admitted he lied about seeing Graham at the gallery the night of the murder," Marcus said. "Said someone paid him to do it, but he doesn't know who. It was all arranged online."

The other officer let out a low whistle. "So someone was trying to frame Graham?"

"Looks that way," Marcus replied. "Whoever it was, they went to a lot of trouble to make sure Graham took the fall."

Lila's heart raced as the implications sank in. One of the crucial pieces of evidence that had pointed to Graham's guilt—his presence near the gallery—had been completely fabricated. Someone had constructed the lie, deliberately diverting suspicion onto an innocent man. Is this what Sam wanted to tell her?

She had been wrong about Graham. The realization sat heavily in her gut, a bitter pill to swallow. She had let herself be led astray, blinded by circumstantial evidence and her own presumptions.

Marcus continued, his voice low and serious. "I spoke with the FBI contact mentioned in those documents Lila brought us. They confirmed Evelyn's involvement in the investigation of the forgery ring."

The other officer leaned in closer, his interest piqued. "So it's true then? She was working with the feds?"

"Yeah," Marcus said, running a hand through his hair. "Evelyn was working alone. No other informants or civilian partners involved."

Lila's breath caught in her throat, her mind reeling with the implications. If Evelyn was working alone, then Maxine's claim of collaboration was a lie.

Marcus continued, his words painting a vivid picture of Evelyn's clandestine work. "Apparently, Evelyn had been gathering evidence for months. She had names, dates, detailed records of transactions. They were on the verge of breaking the whole ring wide open."

Lila's hands trembled as she gripped the steering wheel, her mind racing. The revelation about Graham's innocence and Maxine's lies felt like a physical blow. She had been so certain, so convinced of Graham's guilt, and now...

"How could I have been so blind?" she whispered, her voice barely audible.

The pieces were falling into place with sickening clarity. Maxine's behavior, her evasive answers, the way she had subtly steered suspicion towards Graham - it all pointed to a calculated deception. Lila's stomach churned as she realized how easily she had been manipulated.

She thought back to her confrontation with Maxine in Evelyn's office. The artist's panicked searching, her flimsy excuses, and her reluctance to provide any concrete information now took on a sinister edge. What had Maxine really been looking for? What evidence was she trying to hide or destroy? Was it the papers she had given to Marcus?

Ethan's role in the scheme became clear. As a young, impressionable gallery assistant, he was the perfect target for Maxine. A promise of money, a whispered threat, and he would have been putty in her hands, ready to spin whatever tale she dictated.

Lila's heart sank as she recalled how readily she had accepted Ethan's initial statement, how it had colored her perception of Graham. She had played right into Maxine's hands, allowing herself to be guided by suspicion and doubt.

The realization hit Lila like a tidal wave: Maxine had a motive, means, and opportunity. If Evelyn had uncovered Maxine's participation in the world of art forgeries, it would have been catastrophic. Prison time—Maxine had everything to lose.

Lila's phone buzzed insistently, jolting her from her spiraling thoughts. Sam's name flashed on the screen, a reminder of the urgent message that had pulled her away from the gallery.

Lila answered the call. "Sam? What's going on?"

"Lila, thank God you picked up," Samantha's voice crackled through the speaker, breathless with urgency. "I've got some major news about Graham. You're not going to believe this."

Lila closed her eyes, her free hand gripping the steering wheel tightly. "Let me guess. Ethan lied about seeing Graham at the gallery the night of the murder. Someone paid him to say that, to frame Graham."

There was a moment of stunned silence on the other end of the line. "How... how did you know that?" Samantha stammered.

"I overheard Marcus talking about it just now," Lila explained, her voice heavy with the weight of her realization. "Sam, we were wrong about Graham."

"Lila, this changes everything. If Graham's innocent, then who..."

"I think it was Maxine," Lila cut in, her words tumbling out in a rush. "I caught her searching Evelyn's office, Sam. She was looking for something specific, something she didn't want anyone else to find."

"Maxine?" Sam's voice was incredulous. "Why would she..."

"I don't think they were as close as Maxine wanted us to believe," Lila said, her mind racing. "She just lied to me about working with Evelyn on the forgery investigation. Marcus confirmed with the FBI that Evelyn was working alone."

Lila's thoughts raced as she processed the implications, a nauseating feeling of being betrayed settling in her stomach. She had put her faith in Maxine, shared details of the investigation, never suspecting the very person she confided in was the guilty one.

The weight of the truth settled on Lila's shoulders. She took a deep breath, steeling herself for what lay ahead. There was no turning back now. She had to confront Maxine, had to see this through to the end, no matter how painful it might be.

Lila's heart pounded as she got our of the car and turned back towards the gallery, her steps measured and deliberate. Fear coursed through her veins, the realization that Maxine could be dangerous—even deadly—if backed into a corner. But Lila knew she couldn't walk away, not now, not when the truth was so close.

She paused at the gallery entrance, her hand hovering over the door handle. Inside, Maxine was likely still searching through Evelyn's office. Lila's thoughts were consumed with the impending confrontation, going over all the accusations she would make. She sent a quick message to Marcus to tell him that Maxine was the killer and what she was about to do.

Taking a deep breath, Lila pushed open the door. The gallery was quiet. Lila's footsteps echoed on the polished hardwood as she made her way towards Evelyn's office.

As she approached the office door, Lila could hear the faint murmur of Maxine's voice from within. A phone call, perhaps, or maybe just Maxine talking to herself. Lila just needed to get closer.

Chapter 24

Lila snuck down the dimly lit hallway, her heart pounding in her chest as she approached the slightly ajar door to Evelyn's office. A muffled voice drifted out, and she leaned in, pressing her ear to the crack.

Maxine's agitated tone was unmistakable. "I can't wait any longer. They're closing in on me. I have to get out of town, tonight, before it's too late."

A chill ran down Lila's spine. So it was true. All her suspicions about Maxine's guilt solidified in that moment. She's going to run, Lila realized. And it sounded like she had help.

Lila's thoughts were spinning. She could confront Maxine right away. She could call Marcus. Her curiosity took over. But, she needed to see Maxine's face, to meet her gaze and find out why.

Holding her breath, Lila slowly pushed the door open a fraction in hopes of getting a better view. The old hinges decided then to let out a traitorous creak. Inside, Maxine whirled around, the phone still pressed to her ear.

Their eyes locked. Maxine's flashed with shock, then narrowed. A heavy, tense silence stretched between them for a split second that felt like an eternity. Lila's heart hammered against her ribs as she raised her hands in front of her to try to soothe Maxine.

Maxine's face hardened, her eyes turning to steel as she realized Lila had been eavesdropping. "I have to go," she snapped into the receiver before turning her full attention to Lila. She abruptly ended the call, slamming the phone down. Fear and anger warred in her expression.

Lila slowly entered the office and tried to move to position the desk between herself and Maxine. She swallowed hard, trying to find her voice. "Maxine, I..."

But Maxine cut her off at the front of the desk, positioning herself between Lila and the door. In a flash, she reached into her jacket pocket and pulled out a small, menacing knife. Her hand trembled slightly, betraying her frayed nerves, but the desperation in her eyes was unmistakable.

"You couldn't leave it alone, could you, Lila?" Maxine hissed, advancing on her. Lila stumbled back until she hit the office wall, the cold plaster pressing against her skin. Maxine closed in, the knife held out between them like a deadly accusation. "You just had to keep digging."

Lila's mind raced, searching for a way out, but Maxine was now blocking the only exit. She raised her hands in a placating gesture. "Maxine, please. Let's talk about this."

"Talk?" Maxine let out a humorless laugh, edged with hysteria. As she stepped closer, her voice cracked. "I didn't want to hurt Evelyn! It wasn't supposed to end like this. She was going to ruin me—she found out about the forged paintings, and I... I panicked!"

The words tumbled out in a frantic rush, and Lila's eyes widened as the pieces fell into place. Maxine had been forging paintings. Evelyn had discovered the truth. And in a desperate struggle, Maxine had...

"Let's start from the beginning." Lila asked. "How did this all start?"

Maxine's eyes flickered with a mix of desperation and resignation. She kept the knife pointed at Lila but seemed to deflate slightly, her shoulders sagging under the weight of her secrets.

"It started years ago," Maxine began, her voice barely above a whisper. "I was struggling, barely making ends meet. Evelyn had just opened her gallery, and I... I was desperate for a break. Evelyn took a chance on me, but I needed a sale. So I forged her signature."

Lila's eyes widened, but she remained silent, afraid any interruption might cause Maxine to stop talking.

"Evelyn found out, of course," Maxine continued, her voice bitter. "She was furious. Threatened to expose me, to ruin my career before it even began. That's why she never talked about me, never acknowledged our connection.

"Then I was approached by someone," Maxine continued, her voice trembling. "A collector, or so I thought at first. He offered me a way out, a chance to make real money. All I had to do was recreate a few paintings."

Lila's breath caught in her throat.

"At first, it was just minor works. Small-time artists, nothing too valuable. But then..." Maxine's eyes glazed over, lost in the memory. "Then they asked for a Monet. The money they offered... I couldn't resist."

She let out a bitter laugh. "But Evelyn... she could spot the tiniest inconsistency, the slightest deviation from an artist's true style. When my forged Monet came across her desk as part of a private collection she was appraising, she knew instantly."

Lila listened intently, her heart racing as the full scope of the deception unfolded.

"Evelyn confronted me, of course," Maxine said, her voice resolute. "She was livid. But more than that, she was determined to expose me."

"She threatened to go to the authorities," Maxine continued, her voice trembling. "I begged her not to, tried to explain that it wasn't just me, that there were dangerous people involved. But Evelyn wouldn't listen."

Maxine's grip on the knife tightened, her knuckles turning white. "I started sending her letters, trying to scare her off. Anonymous threats, warnings to back down."

Lila's eyes widened as she recalled the threatening letters that had been found in Evelyn's desk. The pieces were falling into place with sickening clarity.

Lila's mind raced, recalling the legal documents she had discovered. "That's when she went to the FBI," she whispered.

"So you killed her." Lila's voice was barely a whisper, horror and disbelief mingling in her chest. "Evelyn found out, and you killed her to keep your secrets."

Maxine's face crumpled, a tear slipping down her cheek. Her grip on the knife tightened as she moved closer to Lila. "I didn't mean to. But I couldn't let her ruin me."

Lila's heart pumped as she stared at the glinting blade, her mind desperately searching for a way out of this nightmare. She had to find a way to reason with Maxine, to stall her until help could arrive. But with the knife now hovering just inches from her, time was running out.

Maxine's voice quivered as she spoke, a mixture of guilt and desperation. "I never wanted it to come to this, Lila. I never meant to hurt anyone. But Evelyn... she was going to destroy everything I'd worked so hard for."

Lila's mind tried to reconcile the woman she thought she knew with the desperate, cornered figure before her.

Lila's heart clenched. She could see the anguish in Maxine's eyes, the weight of her actions crushing her. But the knife was still there, the threat still real. "Maxine, listen to me. It's not too late. You can still make this right."

Maxine's laugh was bitter, tinged with hopelessness. "Make it right? How? I killed her, Lila. I took her life. There's no coming back from that." Her voice dropped to a whisper. "I didn't mean to kill her... I just wanted to protect myself. But now... I don't know what I'm going to do."

The knife inched closer, and Lila pressed herself against the wall, her heart pounding. She had to keep Maxine talking, had to find a way to break through to her. "Maxine, please. This isn't the answer."

A flicker of doubt crossed Maxine's face, a momentary crack in her resolve. Lila seized the opportunity, her voice urgent. "It's not too late to do the right thing. Please, Maxine. Put down the knife. Let's end this, before it goes any further."

For a heartbeat, Lila thought she'd gotten through to her. But then Maxine's expression hardened, desperation and fear taking over. "No. No, I can't. I won't go to prison."

In a sudden, frantic motion, Maxine shoved Lila aside, sending her stumbling into the desk. Pain shot through Lila's hip as she collided with the edge, but she couldn't focus on that now. Maxine was making a run for it, moving towards the office door.

Lila pushed herself off the desk, ignoring the throbbing ache in her side. She couldn't let Maxine escape, couldn't let her run from the truth. She hurried after her, following the footsteps echoing in the empty gallery.

Maxine was fast, fueled by adrenaline and desperation. She weaved through the exhibits. Lila followed, her breath coming in short gasps, her mind racing.

As Maxine neared the gallery's main entrance, Lila's heart sank. If she made it outside, Maxine would disappear. But then, she heard it. The sound of approaching footsteps outside the front door, the murmur of voices. Someone was coming.

Maxine heard it too. She skidded to a halt, her hand on the door handle, her eyes wide with panic. Lila caught up to her, panting, her voice pleading. "Maxine, don't. It's over. There's nowhere to run."

The footsteps grew louder, closer. Maxine's grip tightened on the handle, her knuckles turning white.

The voices outside grew louder, more distinct. Maxine's hand trembled on the door handle as recognition dawned on her face. "No," she whispered, backing away from the door as if it had suddenly turned red hot.

The door burst open, and Marcus charged in, his gun drawn, flanked by a team of officers. "Police! Freeze!"

Maxine spun around, her face a mask of shock and fear. The knife clattered to the floor as she raised her hands in surrender, tears streaming down her face. "I... I didn't mean to..." Her words came out in broken sobs, her entire body shaking.

Marcus approached her cautiously, his eyes flicking to Lila for a moment, a silent question in his gaze. Lila nodded, her own heart pounding in her chest. It was over. Finally over.

As Marcus holstered his gun and pulled out his handcuffs, Lila let out a shaky breath. She watched as he cuffed Maxine, reading her her rights. The other officers moved in, securing the scene, their radios crackling with static.

Lila leaned against the wall, her legs suddenly feeling like jelly. The adrenaline was wearing off, leaving her exhausted and drained. She couldn't believe it. After all this time, all this searching, it was finally over.

Chapter 25

Lila exhaled deeply, the tension releasing from her shoulders as she watched the officers guide a handcuffed Maxine into the waiting squad car. Her mind reeled, images of Maxine's wild eyes and the glint of the knife replaying in flashes. But now, Lila caught a glimpse of her face. Behind the tears and the fear, there was something else. Something like relief.

Slowly, the adrenaline began to ebb, her heartbeat returning to a steadier rhythm. She was safe now. It was over and she felt as if her legs would no longer hold her up. She leaned against the wall and sunk to the floor.

Footsteps approached and Lila turned to see Marcus, his brow furrowed with concern. Gone was the earlier gruffness in his voice as he asked softly, "You okay?"

Lila nodded, not quite trusting her voice. The reality of what had just occurred, of how close she had come to real harm, crashed over her like a wave. Marcus's warnings echoed in her mind - she had been reckless. If he hadn't arrived when he did…

She shuddered, pushing the thought away and looking up. "I am now. Thank you, Marcus. Really."

He regarded her for a long moment before nodding. "I'm just glad you're alright. But Lila," he fixed her with a pointed look, "no more going rogue like this. It's too dangerous."

"I know. I'm sorry. I thought I could handle it, that I could get through to Maxine…"

"I get it. But leave the detective work to the professionals from now on, okay? I'd hate to see you get hurt." His tone was gentler than she had ever heard it.

Around them, uniformed officers moved about, snapping photos and bagging evidence. The gallery was a hive of activity. Lila watched them work, the chaos a stark contrast to the eerie calm that had fallen between her and Marcus.

She faced him again, really seeing him for perhaps the first time. Beneath the gruff exterior was a man who cared, who believed her when it mattered. Her throat tightened with a swell of emotion. "I owe you one, Detective."

The corner of his mouth quirked. "Let's just call it even. But maybe buy me a coffee sometime and we can talk about keeping you out of trouble."

Despite everything, Lila found herself smiling. "You've got yourself a deal."

Marcus paused, his eyes scanning the room with a detective's keen observation. "We'll need to take a full statement from you, go over everything that happened." His voice was gentle, but there was no mistaking the underlying professionalism.

Lila nodded, exhaustion seeping into her bones. "I understand. Whatever you need." She glanced around at the artwork that lined the walls.

Marcus nodded, giving Lila's shoulder a reassuring squeeze before turning back to the scene. Lila watched as he strode across the gallery, his tall frame cutting a purposeful path through the organized chaos of the crime scene.

As the last police car pulled away, Lila released a shaky breath. The weight of the ordeal pressed down on her, the adrenaline that had kept her going now seeping away. She stood outside the gallery, arms wrapped tightly around herself, warding off the cold. The scene was eerily quiet now, a stark contrast to the chaos mere moments ago.

Lila turned to find Marcus standing quietly beside her, his steady presence a lifeline in the stormy sea of her emotions. "I don't know what I would have done without you," she said softly.

Marcus met her gaze, his blue eyes filled with a softness she hadn't seen before. "You're stronger than you know, Lila. You would have found a way."

She shook her head, a stray tear escaping down her cheek. "No, I mean it. You were there when I needed you, you listened. You stood by me through all of this."

Marcus reached out, his hand gently grasping her shoulder. "That's what partners do." His words were simple, but they carried a depth of meaning that made Lila's heart swell.

She managed a small smile through her tears. "Partners, huh?"

"Well, unofficial partners," he amended with a slight grin. "But I've got your back, Lila. Always."

His words wrapped around her like a warm blanket, providing a sense of safety and comfort she hadn't felt in a long time. She drew in a deep breath, letting it out slowly. "Thank you."

Marcus's hand lingered on her shoulder for a moment before he let it fall away. "Come on," he said gently, "let's get you home. I think your formal statement can wait till tomorrow."

Lila hesitated, her mind swirling with questions. The adrenaline was wearing off, leaving her exhausted.

"Marcus," she began, her voice barely above a whisper, "I have some questions."

He turned to face her, his expression softening. The streetlights cast a warm glow on his face. "Of course, Lila. What do you want to know?"

She took a deep breath, gathering her thoughts. The cool night air filled her lungs. "How did you know about Maxine? How did you know to come here tonight?"

Marcus sighed, running a hand through his hair. He glanced around the now-quiet street, the flashing lights of the departing police cars reflecting off the puddles on the asphalt. "After you brought me those documents, I knew we needed more information. I got in touch with the FBI agent in charge of the forgery investigation."

Marcus continued, his voice low and measured. "The FBI had been working closely with Evelyn for months. She had filled me in on the details of their investigation."

Lila listened intently, her breath catching as Marcus unraveled the intricate web of deceit.

"According to them, the forgery ring Evelyn uncovered wasn't just a local operation. It stretched across multiple states, maybe even internationally."

Marcus's words hung heavy in the night air, sending a chill down Lila's spine. She gazed out at the quiet street, her mind reeling with the enormity of what they had uncovered.

"So it wasn't just Maxine," Lila breathed, her voice growing more steady. "There could be others out there?"

Marcus nodded grimly. "Yes, there are others, and unfortunately now we may not catch them."

Lila nodded and allowed him to guide her to his car, sinking into the passenger seat with a heavy sigh. As Marcus navigated the quiet streets of Willow Creek, she stared out the window, watching the familiar storefronts and houses blur past.

Chapter 26

The gallery hummed with a quiet energy as Lila stepped through the glass doors. She was met with an equal feeling of joy and togetherness. Conversations flowed, glasses clinked, and the faint strains of a string quartet drifted through the air.

Lila's eyes scanned the room, taking in the sea of faces—some familiar, some new. The walls were adorned with an eclectic mix of artwork, each piece telling a unique story. Delicate floral arrangements and flickering candles were interspersed throughout, adding a personal touch that felt like a loving tribute to Evelyn.

As she wove through the crowd, Lila caught snippets of conversations:

"Did you see Adrian's latest piece? It's stunning!"

"I heard the proceeds from tonight are going to the new arts foundation in Evelyn's name."

"The turnout is incredible. Evelyn would be so proud."

Lila's heart swelled with a mix of emotions. Pride for her and Adrian's success, gratitude for the community's support, and a bittersweet ache for the absence of her friend and mentor. She paused in front of a large abstract painting.

Samantha stood in the center of the gallery, surrounded by the lively buzz of people. Lila spotted her amongst the crowd and approached her. Her friend's posture was proud, yet there was a glimmer of sadness in her eyes as she surveyed the bustling crowd. Lila wove her way through the throng of people, her skirt swishing against her legs, until she reached Samantha's side.

"Sam, the show is a hit. You did it," Lila said warmly, her blue eyes sparkling with admiration as she gestured toward the lively gathering.

Samantha turned to face Lila, a smile blossoming on her face as she accepted the compliment. Relief danced in her eyes, the weight of the event's success finally settling on her shoulders. "I didn't do it alone. I've had help. And you and Adrian are the stars," she admitted, her voice laced with gratitude.

Lila reached out, giving Samantha's hand a gentle squeeze. She knew how much this moment meant to her friend, how tirelessly they had worked to keep Evelyn's vision alive.

Samantha's expression shifted, a flicker of determination crossing her features as she met Lila's gaze. "I've decided to buy the gallery," she revealed, her voice steady with conviction. "I'll keep it running as the Evelyn Grey Gallery, in her honor."

Lila's heart swelled with pride, a mixture of emotions welling up inside her. She knew the sacrifices Samantha had made, the long hours she had poured into keeping the gallery afloat in the wake of Evelyn's passing. This decision was more than just a business venture; it was a tribute to the woman who had mentored them both, who had believed in the power of art.

Samantha's lips curved into a playful grin, a mischievous glint in her eye. "Who knows, I may even look into that merger with Graham," she quipped, her tone light and teased.

Lila couldn't help but chuckle at the thought, the tension between Evelyn and the other gallery owner suddenly seeming insignificant at the moment.

As the laughter faded, a sense of peace settled over Lila. With Samantha at the helm, the Evelyn Grey

Gallery would remain a beacon of creativity and inspiration, a testament to the unforgettable mark Evelyn had left on the town's art scene.

"She'd be proud of you, Sam," Lila whispered, her voice thick with emotion. "This is exactly what she would have wanted."

Samantha nodded, her eyes glistening with unshed tears. "I know," she murmured, her hand finding Lila's once more. "And I promise to make her proud every single day."

As the evening went on, the gallery was filled with excited chatter as people gathered around Adrian's and Lila's works. Filled with raw emotion, conversations hummed in admiration for their intense and profound paintings.

Lila watched from a distance, her keen eyes taking in the scene. Adrian stood near his largest painting, a towering canvas that seemed to pulse with energy. His dark hair fell rakishly over his brow as he engaged in animated discussions with the guests, his passion for his work evident in every gesture.

As if sensing her gaze, Adrian looked up, his eyes locking with hers across the crowded gallery. For a fleeting instant, the world seemed to fall away, leaving just the two of them, connected by an unspoken understanding. In that moment, Lila saw a flicker of vulnerability beneath his confident exterior, a glimpse of the man behind the artist. She nodded.

Adrian returned the nod, his features softening into a smile that was equal parts relief and gratitude. In that moment, Lila felt a surge of pride and affection for her friend. She knew how much this night meant to Adrian - a chance to showcase his talent, to prove himself worthy of Evelyn's legacy. And as she watched the admiring crowds gather around his work, she had no doubt that he had succeeded.

"He's really something, isn't he?" a voice beside her remarked, pulling Lila from her thoughts. She turned to find a well-dressed woman, her eyes fixed on Adrian's paintings. "I've never seen anything quite like it. The emotion... it's breathtaking."

Lila nodded, a smile playing on her lips. "He's a true talent," she agreed, her voice warm with admiration. "And he's worked incredibly hard to get here. It's been a long road, but he never gave up."

The woman turned to face Lila, her expression curious. "You know him well?"

"We're friends," Lila replied, her gaze drifting back to Adrian, who was now engaged in an animated conversation with a group of admirers.

As the night progressed, the gallery continued to thrum with energy, a celebration of art and community. Lila's eyes scanned the bustling gallery, taking in the vibrant energy of the crowd. Amidst the laughter and chatter, her gaze settled on a familiar figure standing alone in a quieter corner. Graham Whitaker, his posture stiff and his expression pensive, nursed a drink as he observed the scene from a distance.

Lila hesitated for a moment, recalling the tension that had lingered between them throughout the investigation. But as she watched Graham, she felt a pang of sympathy. Steeling herself, she made her way through the throng of people.

As she approached, Graham looked up, his eyes widening slightly in surprise. Lila met his gaze, her own expression a mix of determination and contrition. "Graham," she began, her voice soft but clear above the hum of conversation, "I owe you an apology."

Graham's brow furrowed, but he remained silent, allowing her to continued. Lila took a deep breath, the words tumbling out in a rush. "I shouldn't have assumed you could have been involved in Evelyn's death. I was wrong."

For a long moment, Graham simply stared at her, his face unreadable. Then, slowly, he nodded, a flicker of understanding in his eyes. "I know why you believed it," he said, his voice low and measured. "Evelyn and I had our issues, not to mention that argument in front of everyone. But honestly, without your persistence, I might've ended up arrested."

Lila felt a wave of relief wash over her, the tension between them beginning to dissipate. She watched as Graham's shoulders relaxed, his grip on his glass loosening. "You helped uncover the truth, and in the end, I think she was trying to protect me and my reputation" he continued, his tone softening. "I can't hold that against you."

Graham's gaze drifted to one of Lila's paintings hanging nearby. His expression softened, a flicker of admiration crossing his features. "You know," he began, his voice tinged with a hint of regret, "I owe you an apology as well."

Lila tilted her head, curiosity piqued. Graham took a sip of his drink, gathering his thoughts before continuing. "Those comments I made about your work, before my argument with Evelyn... I was out of line."

He gestured towards her painting. "The truth is, your work is extraordinary. It's truly remarkable."

Lila felt a warmth spread through her chest at his words, unexpected but deeply appreciated. Graham continued, his voice low and sincere. "I was just trying to get under Evelyn's skin that day. I knew how proud she was of you. I thought if I criticized you, it would rile her up."

A small smile tugged at the corners of Lila's mouth, a silent acknowledgment of the newfound respect that had blossomed between them. As they parted ways, each returning to their own orbits within the gallery, Lila couldn't help but feel a sense of closure. As she wove her way back through the crowd, Lila's heart felt lighter, unburdened by the weight of suspicion and mistrust.

The hum of conversations mingled with the soft clink of glasses, creating a symphony of togetherness that warmed her heart. She watched as people gathered around the showcased artwork. In that moment, Lila couldn't help but feel a swell of pride for herself and her fellow artist.

Her gaze drifted to Samantha, who was still near the center of the room, engaged in an animated discussion with a group of patrons. The decision to take over the gallery had been a bold one, but as Lila watched her friend's confident gestures and bright smile, she knew that it had been the right choice. Samantha's passion for art and her dedication to honoring Evelyn's legacy would ensure that the gallery would continue to thrive.

As everything began to wind down and the crowd started to thin, Lila's attention was drawn to a familiar figure standing quietly by the door. Marcus, his hands clasped behind his back, observed the scene with a calm, contemplative expression. Their eyes met across the room, and Lila felt a flicker of understanding pass between them.

She raised her hand in a small wave, a smile playing on her lips. Marcus returned the gesture, his own expression softening into something warm and unguarded. In that brief, silent exchange, Lila felt a sense of gratitude wash over her, despite their occasional disagreements and Marcus's initial skepticism.

As the moment passed and Marcus turned his attention back to the remaining guests, Lila felt a sense of closure settle over her. The truth had been uncovered, justice had been served, and the community had come together in a beautiful display of support. And through it all, she had discovered a strength within herself that she hadn't known existed.

With a final glance around the gallery, taking in the art, the people, and the love that filled the space, Lila knew that Evelyn's legacy would live on.

This is my debut novel.

But don't worry, there is more to come!

*Sign Up for My
Newsletter!*